ROCKY ROAD
AHEAD

ROCKY ROAD
AHEAD

Coco Simon

Simon Spotlight

New York   London   Toronto   Sydney   New Delhi

SIMON SPOTLIGHT
An imprint of Simon & Schuster Children's Publishing Division
1230 Avenue of the Americas, New York, New York 10020
This Simon Spotlight edition May 2019
Copyright © 2019 by Simon & Schuster, Inc.
All rights reserved, including the right of reproduction in whole or in part in any form.
SIMON SPOTLIGHT and colophon are registered trademarks of Simon & Schuster, Inc.
For information about special discounts for bulk purchases, please contact Simon & Schuster
Special Sales at 1-866-506-1949 or business@simonandschuster.com.
Text by Elizabeth Doyle Carey
Series cover design by Alisa Coburn and Hannah Frece
Cover design by Laura Roode
Cover illustrations by Alisa Coburn
Series interior design by Hannah Frece
The text of this book was set in Bembo Std.
Manufactured in the United States of America 0419 OFF
10 9 8 7 6 5 4 3 2 1
ISBN 978-1-5344-4042-5 (hc)
ISBN 978-1-5344-4041-8 (pbk)
ISBN 978-1-5344-4043-2 (eBook)
Library of Congress Catalog Card Number 2019937279

CHAPTER ONE
YAY GOURMET!

It was the after-lunch rush on a beautiful Sunday afternoon. That was about as busy as Molly's Ice Cream shop ever got, and I loved it! I felt so good when we were busy—my friends Tamiko and Sierra and me moving smoothly behind the counter like a well-oiled machine, the register ringing and ringing sales, and "inventory" (as my mom called our ice cream and toppings) moving out the door. Most of all, I loved happy customers, and today we had plenty!

There was a group of Girl Scouts coming back from a campout—they wanted to be refreshed, so we sold them a lot of sorbet. There were grandparents babysitting grandchildren, and they always went big: unicorn sundaes, candy toppings, hot fudge. All the stuff parents usually forbade, the grandparents bought. Putting together the more complicated items on the menu satisfied our creativity as scoopers. After all, it was more fun to create a fancy mermaid sundae than it was to put a scoop of vanilla ice cream into a cone, even if it *was* rich, creamy, delicious Molly's Ice Cream vanilla!

My friends and I were in the middle of serving a car pool of Little Leaguers when I noticed that my mom had come into the front of the store from her office in the back. Her eyes were bright with excitement, and her cheeks were pink. She looked like she had news of some sort. I wanted to stop what I was doing and run over to her to talk, but we were too overwhelmed. The line was out the door. I was alternating between scooping and running the register, which meant I couldn't break for even one second.

I kept my eye on her as we worked through the rush. She went back to her office and returned with her laptop in hand right as the line was drawing to an end. I caught her eye, and she grinned widely at me. Phew! That meant she definitely had good news. I was so eager to chat with her that I rushed as I packed a scoop into a cone, and I cracked it and had to start over. Ice cream was the ultimate slow food—there was just no way to rush making it, serving it, or eating it!

Finally, finally, things died down and I darted over to my mom.

"What's going on?" I asked breathlessly. "You look so excited!"

My mom smiled again and threw her arm around me in a sideways hug. "We're going to be famous!" she said with a laugh.

I laughed too, just because she was so happy. "How? Why?"

By now Tamiko and Sierra had wiped down the counters and joined us.

"Girls, I just got a wonderful e-mail from a reporter at *Yay Gourmet*, the online food magazine!"

"*Yay Gourmet!*" Tamiko squealed. "I love them! Their site is supercool, and amazing at predicting new food trends."

"And what did the e-mail say?' Sierra asked.

My mom beamed proudly. "They want to do a big article about Molly's!"

"Awesome!" Sierra and I exclaimed together.

Tamiko clapped her hands. "What are they going to focus on in the article?"

My mom tipped her head to the side thoughtfully. "I think our flavors most of all. Then our technique—the small batches, the high-quality ingredients, the test kitchen where I create them all. But there will certainly be a section on the wonderful concoctions you girls have created: the sundaes, shakes, and—"

"And the sprinkle of happy?" Sierra and I chimed.

My mom laughed. "Of course! What would Molly's be without a sprinkle of happy?"

A sprinkle of happy was something that I had invented in the early days of the store last year, right when we'd all started working together every Sunday. No matter how plain or complicated the ice cream order, we put a pinch of rainbow sprinkles on top and said to the customer, "Here's your sprinkle of happy!" People loved it. It always, *always* made them smile.

"When will the article run?" asked Tamiko. She was always one for the details.

"I'm not sure of the exact date," said my mom. "But I definitely think early summer. The reporter mentioned publishing it right in time for 'ice cream season.'"

4

Tamiko wrinkled her nose. "Don't they know it's *always* ice cream season at Molly's?"

Sierra and I laughed. Tamiko was a marketing whiz, and she was always trying to think of new ways to attract customers and attention—promotions, flyers, special events, social media, new menu items. She was a one-girl publicity machine, and Molly's had a lot to thank her for, especially building our fan base and attracting and keeping customers.

"We will make sure the reporter knows that before she leaves the store," said my mom with a nod of agreement. "Ice cream's not just for summer anymore!"

My two friends and I went back to our spots behind the counter and began straightening up the chaos that our busy hour and a half had created. Sierra topped off the pots of sprinkles, cherries, nuts, and candies. Tamiko restocked cones, napkins, and cups. I refilled the crocks with marshmallow, hot fudge, and caramel (a sticky task!). As we worked, we discussed our summer plans.

"I can't believe it's right around the corner again!" said Sierra.

"I know. I've got to line up some activities," I agreed.

5

"Are you going back to your sleepaway camp again?" Tamiko asked me.

I shrugged. "I'm not really sure. Things are different this summer, since . . ."

My friends knew what I meant—since my parents' divorce. At the end of the previous summer I had come back from my happy place (sleepaway camp) to discover that my parents were getting divorced and it was a done deal. They were both moving to new places, my brother and I were going to new schools, and my mom was switching to a new job, which was opening Molly's.

It had been a year of big changes and a lot more responsibility for me. But I also had much more independence now because of it. I got to work at Molly's; I sometimes took care of my brother, Tanner, and got us both dinner and off to bed; and my parents trusted me to get around on my own more than they used to. Also, both of my parents now lived in supercool, very different places that I loved, and I'd been able to start at an awesome new school. I still missed my old school—especially because Tamiko and Sierra were there without me—but I liked a lot of things about my new school too, like the librarian, Mrs. K.; and my English teacher, Ms. Healy; and being on the school paper; and my new friend Colin. Even the food was better at my new school.

Tamiko and Sierra and I had figured out how to stay close even though we went to different schools, and that included lots of video chats; working together every Sunday, rain or shine; and plenty of fun plans when we could fit them in.

But summer was still a big question mark. Would my mom need my help at home, watching Tanner, working at the store, or whatever? Would my dad want to spend more time together over the summer? Could we afford for me to go to that fancy camp up north for seven weeks again? We hadn't discussed it yet, but I wasn't even sure I *wanted* to go again. I almost hoped they'd make the decision for me. Or I hoped that maybe something better would come along.

"What about you, Sierra? Do you have summer plans?" I asked.

Sierra screwed the plastic lid back onto the giant jar of rainbow sprinkles and stowed the jar back in the cabinet. She turned to us and said, "Isa and I are going to work for our parents a bunch at their clinic. I'd love to work at Molly's, too. Maybe I could pick up some more shifts, what with summer being the busy season and me being free to help more."

I nodded. "That would be fun. The time will fly in here this summer because it'll be crowded every day. What about you, Miko? Do you have a plan?"

"I have some DIY projects up my sleeve. I might set up a table at the weekly flea market in the town square and sell some of my crafts and creations. Then my dad's talking about us all going to Japan in August to see my grandfather. I'd really be psyched to go," she said as she artfully created a pyramid display of cups of all sizes.

I clapped my hands. "Ooooh! That would be awesome! And maybe you could do some ice cream research there!"

"I know," said Tamiko, nodding. "Like the taiyaki!"

Taiyaki cones were little fish-shaped cakes that got filled with ice cream and dipped in fudge and sprinkles for decoration. Tamiko had introduced them to my mom, and we were considering introducing them to our menu at some point.

"I'm sure you could learn new ice cream ideas

without having to go all the way to Japan," offered Sierra as a new group of customers entered the store. "Welcome to Molly's!" she greeted them cheerfully, and we were off and running again.

After our shift was over, my mom told us each to help ourselves to a free treat since it had been such a busy day. I asked if we could please borrow her laptop to look at the *Yay Gourmet* site while we relaxed, and she agreed, donning an apron and washing her hands to cover the pre-dinner lull before things heated up again later.

Sitting at a table in the far corner, we each indulged in our current favorite Molly's item. Tamiko was having a Coconut Cake sundae—coconut ice cream with yellow cake crumbles and real shredded coconut topping mixed in, all covered in a heavy pour of liquid marshmallow. Sierra had a simple dish of lemon sorbet in front of her. She'd felt tired and overheated and wanted to be refreshed just like the Girl Scouts. I was hungry, so I'd gone for something a little more satisfying, a Rockin' Rocky Road cone that was crunchy, salty, and sweet.

Tamiko pulled up the *Yay Gourmet* site and began

surfing around. Sierra and I scooted our chairs closer to her so that we could all look at the site together. It was such a pretty website, with a cool, puffy logo (it looked like it had been made by a balloon artist) and brightly colored feature articles with mouthwatering close-up photos and lots of handwritten notes and callouts with arrows. It made food look like the most fun thing on earth, which it kind of was!

"They have a cool take on food reporting," said Tamiko admiringly, scrolling down.

I nodded. "Yeah. It's like an annotated cookbook that a chef has had for years. Look at 'Chunky Chuck Wagon Chilis.'"

"And 'Crazy Potato Chip Flavors You Can Make at Home'!" said Sierra with a laugh, pointing at a sidebar. "I'm getting hungry!"

"What will they say about Molly's, I wonder?" I said.

"'Artisanal Ice Cream Made by Geniuses'!" said Tamiko.

"'Made by *Beautiful* Geniuses'!" corrected Sierra.

We laughed.

"Or how about 'Beautiful, Well-Read Geniuses'?" I said.

"'Beautiful, Stylish Geniuses'?" Tamiko questioned.

"'Beautiful, Talented Geniuses.' That's it!" Sierra sang out.

As our laughter subsided, we took bites of our ice cream while Tamiko clicked around on the site. Suddenly I felt a tiny bit of nervousness creep in.

"I hope they say nice things about Molly's," I said.

"Oh, please. How could they not?" said Tamiko with a shrug.

I raised my eyebrows. "Well, you never know. I mean, it's a free press. They could say anything about us."

"It's not really a *review* site, though," said Sierra. "It's not like the local paper, here to give us only one star or something."

"Hey! The local paper gave us five stars! The most we could get!" I pretended to look offended.

"Down, girl!" said Tamiko through a mouthful of coconut. "It's food news. And we've got plenty of *new* stuff going on here for them to write about. Get it? *NEWS*?"

"I guess," I said.

Sierra patted my back. "Don't worry. It's gonna be great."

CHAPTER TWO
LARD & GLUE

I smacked my forehead as I stood waiting for the school bus Monday morning. I'd forgotten to ask my mom if it would be okay for me to tell people about the *Yay Gourmet* article. I mean, I'd told my dad when he and Tanner had come to pick me up for dinner after work at Molly's, but Dad was family.

The person I was most excited to tell was Colin, my school bus buddy and probably my closest friend at Vista Green, my new school (which wasn't that new to me anymore). He was an editor of the school paper—actually, the person who'd encouraged me to join it in the first place—and I knew he'd be interested in the *NEWS*, as Tamiko had called it.

The bus pulled up, and I climbed aboard, scanning the crowd. I found Colin sitting in one of our usual spots toward the back right. I passed the Mean Team—Blair, Palmer, and Maria—near the front and didn't even flick my eyes toward them. One on one, Maria could be okay, but Blair and Palmer were awful, and as a threesome they were intolerable. Colin had helped me deal with them right from the start.

Now Colin was smiling and waving me back. I smiled in return and beelined toward him, then flopped into the seat and dropped my heavy backpack to the floor.

"Good weekend?" he asked by way of greeting.

I tipped my head. "Weekends are always good. Better than weekdays, for sure."

He nodded, smiling. "Totally. What did you do?"

I filled him in on my weekend, which didn't end up sounding that interesting because the one piece of information I was dying to share had to be carefully left out. Colin had had a decent weekend, but he'd had a lot to write and edit for the paper.

"You should consider writing more articles in the newspaper," Colin said. "My sister always says that you're the strongest writer on the staff."

I blushed. "Your older sister? The one who goes to high school?"

Colin laughed. "The one and only!"

"How does she know my writing?"

"I always bring home the school paper, and since she writes for the high school paper, she always checks it out. She loves your ice-cream-and-book pairings every week and says you're a really strong writer."

"Huh!" I sat back in my seat and looked away, pleased.

"She says most of my friends write well, but you stand out."

I turned to look back at him. "How does she know we're friends?" I blurted, then regretted it as Colin blushed and looked out the window.

"Oh, I've just mentioned you at home. You know."

I knew. I'd mentioned Colin at home too. My family had known him first as "the boy who was nice on the bus my first day," and then as "the boy who got me involved with the school paper," and finally as "my friend Colin."

"My family knows you're my friend too," I offered.

"Thanks!" he said, turning to look at me. Then he squinted at my head. "New headband?"

I *was* wearing a new headband—brown with white polka dots—but I couldn't believe he'd noticed.

"Yes! What do you think?" I asked, jokingly making a fish face and tilting my head at all angles like a model.

He laughed. "Headband-y," he said.

I punched him in the arm, not hard. "That's not even a word!"

"No, no, it's nice. You look good," he said, smiling and meeting my eyes.

I smiled and looked down as my cheeks grew pink. "Thanks."

When I went to the bathroom in between classes, I took an extra long look at myself in the new headband, turning my head back and forth and not caring who saw. Colin had liked the way it looked, and that had given me a new perspective. I'd never thought of him as someone who'd notice what I was wearing. Maybe being a newspaper editor made a person more observant or something.

Later, walking down to the library after lunch, I spied my reflection in one of its huge glass walls, and I caught myself smiling as I walked toward my own image. I had to laugh. I was acting like one of the Mean Girls myself, smiling at my own reflection!

I had twelve minutes before my next class, and I wanted to say hi to Mrs. K., the librarian and also my favorite staff member at school. I also wanted to take a minute to look at some food magazines, if the library had any.

"Hi, Mrs. K.!" I whispered as I entered.

"Oh, yes. Mm-hmm. Hello, dear. I know I have something here for you. Let's see." Mrs. K. rummaged through some small, neat piles on her full but tidy desk. She was always a fashion plate. Today she was wearing a boatneck navy-and-white-striped cotton sweater with long sleeves, navy capri pants, and black ballet flats, with her long, dark hair in a ponytail.

"I like your outfit," I whispered.

"Thank you, dear. Feeling summery! Aha! Here we go. Yes." She handed me a stack of cookbooks. "Could you please shelve these for me? They're in one of your sections."

"Okay." I helped Mrs. K. maintain the bookshelves in our library. I was a volunteer, but it never felt like work for me. The library had been my haven when I'd first started at Vista Green, and I'd do anything to give back. "Do you have any cooking magazines?" I added.

"Mm-hmm. Right over there at the far left of the periodical wall. Not a lot. Just some for the kitchen staff and our foodie teachers. Take a peek."

"Thanks." I crossed the plush rug that helped hush the room, heading first to unload the cookbooks. There were only seven of them, and it was a small section, so it wouldn't take more than a minute. But midway through the stack, one of them caught my eye. It was called *Professional Food Photography*, and it had a photo of an ice cream sundae on the cover! I had to check this book out myself.

Quickly I shelved the last two books, and then I went to look at the periodical wall. Unfortunately, periodicals couldn't be checked out—they were too vulnerable to ripping—so I grabbed three magazines and sat in an armchair to flip through them for my remaining time.

The first one was for casual cooks looking for shortcuts—time-saving, money-saving, environment-saving recipes galore. It wasn't really what I was looking for. The next one was a major gourmet magazine featuring complicated multipart recipes that called for people to make their own ingredients first (like homemade mayonnaise and chicken stock). Bor-ing! But the third magazine was a little edgier, closer to *Yay Gourmet*'s style, and interesting, too.

Inside were articles like I'd seen on the website the day before, many of them featuring gourmet shops and restaurants from around the country. The magazine would do a little profile of the chef or owner of a store and then talk about the menu and the recipes. I kept flipping through the magazine and somehow ended up on the Letters to the Editors page. My eyes widened.

Three of the six letters were from people who wanted corrections to the articles about their business. One mentioned a recipe that had been misquoted and had resulted in a disgusting dish. Another letter said that the magazine had misquoted her. And a third said the magazine had "willfully maligned" her business, which I took to mean criticized it too much. Eek.

After each letter the magazine's editors apologized. I supposed it was good that they admitted their mistakes and published them like this, but still. How many people had seen the original articles and been misled? How many of those would ever see the corrections?

I sat back in my chair and stared into space. My mom would have to be very careful about what she said in her *Yay Gourmet* interview. So would my friends and I. I wouldn't want Molly's to be a victim of these sorts of reporting errors. I was still superexcited for Mom, but now I felt a little nervous about releasing Molly's to the world on the internet and having no control over what was said about it. Maybe it was better to be small and *not* well known, if at least you could be sure you were in control of what was being said about you or your business.

The bell rang, and I quickly returned the magazines to the display area and presented the food photography book to Mrs. K. to check out. After a wave and a promise to return the next day, I dashed to my math class, the book clutched under my arm.

Math was fine, but I was distracted by the things I'd read in the library and was also eager to start flipping through the food photography book I now had. By the end of class I was counting the hours until I could go home.

"Hey, Allie," said a voice.

I looked up from repacking my backpack. It was Patrick Ryan, a boy whose birthday party I'd been at the previous weekend. Sierra's new band had been playing at the party because the drummer, Reagan, was Patrick's cousin. Sierra had invited Tamiko and me and her twin, Isabel, so that we could see her play, and there'd turned out to be lots of kids there from Vista Green—including Colin! It had been really fun.

"Hey, Patrick! I've been hoping to run into you to say thanks for the party the other night."

"Thanks for coming! Small world, right?"

"Totally!" I agreed.

Patrick and I strolled out of math class and realized we were headed in the same direction, so we chatted as we walked.

"The Wildflowers are awesome, don't you think?" I asked. That was the name of Sierra's band.

"Yeah. I really couldn't believe it. I mean, Reagan's always been musical, but to see them come together so well, it was impressive." Then Patrick glanced at me. "Are you friends with Tessa, who writes the songs? The one who likes Colin?"

20

Wait, *what*? My heart skipped a beat. Tessa was the guitarist in the Wildflowers, and Sierra had told me that she had a crush on Colin. But how did Patrick know about it?

"Um . . . n-no?" I stuttered. Then I added awkwardly: "She seems nice?"

"Uh-huh. I only talked with her a little bit, but she seems supercool, don't you think?"

"Oh, yeah. I . . . barely met her."

"She and Colin would make a cute couple. I'll have to dream up some other reason to have a party with a band so that we can get those two together again." Patrick stopped outside the science lab. "Well, this is me! See you next time we have math!"

My head was spinning. Did Colin know about Tessa's feelings? Did he like her back?

I sighed. Not that it mattered who Colin liked. Right?

But if so, then why did my conversation with Patrick leave such a bitter taste in my mouth?

Colin had chess after school that day, so he wasn't on my bus home, thankfully. I was having trouble processing this new image of Colin and Tessa as a possible couple. It didn't match with the Colin who'd made me feel so good about my headband that morning. I was feeling . . . weird, I guess. I flipped through the food photography book on the bus a little bit, but I couldn't read it while we were in motion, or I'd get carsick.

Once I was home, though, I curled up on the window seat in my room—a window seat never got old—and I read through the photo book with my cat, Diana. But what I learned made me even more nervous about the *Yay Gourmet* feature than I'd been before!

It turned out that food photographers used lots of tricks of the trade to make food—or should I say "food"—look appealing. For example, droplets of milk were often actually white glue. Chicken breasts were often painted by hand to make grill marks. Stylists used red lipstick to brighten strawberries and mashed potatoes to thicken milkshakes. Worst of all, vanilla ice cream was usually just white lard—animal fat—scooped from a bucket with an ice cream scooper. *Ugh*. Talk about unappetizing!

The book said that ice cream was the hardest thing of all to photograph because it melted under the lights. As soon as you got something that looked delicious and perfect, you had to light it with hot studio lights, and everything melted!

At that, I closed the book in disgust.

Scoops of lard at Molly's?

Never!

CHAPTER THREE
ANNE'S ADVICE

At breakfast the next morning I remembered to ask my mom when I could tell people about the *Yay Gourmet* article.

"Oh, sweetie, I'm so glad you're excited!" she said. "But let's keep it between all of us at least until the reporter comes. That way we know for sure that they're doing it, and we'll have a feel for when it will run. I'd hate to tell people about it and then not have it come out."

"Hmm," I said. I knew she was right, but keeping it a secret was going to be easier said than done!

I felt awkward and nervous that morning on the bus with Colin, now that I was thinking of him and Tessa as a "cute couple." I couldn't help but take everything he said the wrong way.

"Are you going away this summer?" he asked.

And I heard: "Will you be around to see me start dating Tessa?"

"What are you and your friends doing this weekend?" he asked.

And I heard: "It's nice that you have friends to do things with, since you don't have a boyfriend."

"Have you heard the new song by Beyoncé?" he asked.

And I heard: "I'm really into bands and singer-songwriters right now . . . especially Tessa."

By the end of the bus ride, I was totally grumpy. Colin did seem a little perplexed when I huffed off the bus and down the hall to class with barely a goodbye, but what could I have said? *I* wasn't even sure why I was so grumpy.

Unfortunately, I had a newspaper meeting scheduled for lunchtime that day . . . and it was run by Colin. There was no escaping him! I considered skipping it, but I was still new enough that I was low on the newspaper totem pole, and I didn't want to risk missing an assignment. Also, I liked the other kids on the paper, and hanging out and talking shop with them was fun. These meetings were one of the main ways I'd made some friends and fit in a little at Vista Green.

Colin called the meeting to order.

"Any feedback on last week's articles?" he asked the assembled group.

Tom, one of the oldest kids on the paper, groaned. "We had an error in the school lunch article," he said.

"Oh no! What was it?" asked Sara, the managing editor. She was in charge of all the proofreading, and she worked with our designer to make sure all the articles were laid out neatly and not cut off.

"Actually, it was a factual error," said Tom.

"Even worse!" said Colin, smacking his forehead. "What was it?"

"We said that the kitchen lady we profiled was new this year, but she has actually worked here for six years!"

"That's not *so* bad," I said, trying to ease his unhappiness. "I thought you were going to say something really awful."

Tom looked at me in surprise. "But don't you see? It's basically saying we never noticed her before!"

26

I felt everyone staring at me. Why had I opened my mouth? "Oh" was all I could say. My cheeks were starting to burn, and I tried to will the blush to stop rising, but it didn't work.

"We'll need to run a correction," said Colin briskly.

Sara nodded and made a note on her legal pad.

Then Colin cleared his throat. "Does anyone have any good ideas for feature articles?"

The room was silent. People looked around at one another expectantly, then down at their laps. Some people fiddled with the cuffs of their jeans, or picked at their fingernails.

"Has anyone *read* any good feature articles anywhere lately? Something that might inspire us? I'm not saying we'd copy the idea, but maybe it could spark something?" said Colin. He looked searchingly at us all; no one was willing to expose themselves by going first.

Colin looked frustrated, and even though I was annoyed at him at that moment, I hated to see my friend suffer.

"I . . . uh . . ." I gave a little cough. I knew Mom didn't want me to talk about it yet, but I really wanted to give Colin an idea. "Molly's Ice Cream is going to be featured on a famous website soon. Maybe we can reprint the website's article in our newspaper?"

Suddenly there was an excited buzz in the room.

"Awesome!"

"That place has the best ice cream."

"Which website is it?" asked Colin.

"Or is it top secret until it's published?" another staff writer added.

I hesitated. "Um, I'm actually not allowed to say until they've scheduled it to run."

"Well," Colin continued, "when will the article run, then?"

"Umm . . . I'm not exactly sure," I admitted.

Colin let out a tiny sigh. "We'll need more information before we can decide on anything. Also, I don't think we can just reprint something that we didn't write ourselves. It could be like plagiarism and become a whole big copyright mess."

I ducked my head, nodding. "Right. Sorry," I said. Now my cheeks *were* blazing, and there was nothing I could do about it.

However, my offering had broken the ice, and now ideas were whizzing around the room.

"How about something on bake sales?"

"Why are our dances so boring?"

"We need new bike racks!"

"What about the new crossing guard?"

And so on.

Meanwhile, I was annoyed at how Colin had immediately poked holes in the idea I had pitched. I mean, I'd been trying to bail him out! No one else had been suggesting anything, and I'd warmed up the crowd. He could have handled my idea a little better. I felt grumpy and embarrassed.

"What about profiling some of the musicians in school?" asked Winnie, a seventh grader.

There was some more buzz, and heads started nodding.

"I know, like, four or five people who'd be really good. A cellist, a guitarist, a sixth grader who sings in an a cappella group," continued Winnie.

Colin was nodding. "I like it. Maybe a musician of the week?"

Winnie's cheeks turned pink with pride. "Sure! I'd love to do that!"

"Great. Why don't you pull together a list of people? Maybe check to see that they're willing to be interviewed first. Then we'll get that ball rolling. Okay?" Colin beamed at Winnie.

Grr! Why was he being so nice to her? I was supposed to be his friend! He was supposed to like all *my* ideas!

"Great. Thanks!" agreed Winnie. "I'm excited—so many musicians work so hard, and we have no idea that they even have these amazing talents."

Colin nodded. "I know what you mean. I have a friend who goes to a different school, and she's really good at the guitar. She even writes her own songs. But she doesn't perform very often, so most people have no idea about her hidden talent."

My stomach churned. Of course he was talking about Tessa.

"Her own songs? That's so cool!" said Winnie.

"Anyway, I can't wait to read your first article!" Colin continued, and Winnie blushed happily again. "What else have we got?"

I was seething inside. I wasn't about to offer up any more ideas for him to punch holes in, and then watch while he got all jazzed about someone else's idea. Especially when that idea made him think of Tessa!

I almost stood up and left, but I didn't have a good enough excuse, and I didn't want people to think I'd left just because I'd had to go to the bathroom really badly or something. So I stuck it out, and when the meeting wrapped up shortly after, I bolted. Normally I would have hung around and chatted with some of the other newspaper kids, but not that day. I went right to the bathroom and tried to video-chat Tamiko and Sierra for comfort.

But they weren't picking up. Maybe MLK had an assembly during lunch or something. Whatever it was, I suddenly felt very, very alone.

Colin was my closest friend at Vista Green, and my two real besties were together somewhere without me.

The day stank.

I suffered through the rest of the day, waited until Colin had left on the early bus, and then rode home on the late bus with a bunch of sixth graders who were back from a science field trip to the wetlands. They were still all wound up and making birdcalls across the bus for the whole ride home. It was the ultimate punishment for the end of the day.

I got off the bus and trudged home, where I found my mom making an early dinner before she popped back over to the test kitchen to work on two new flavors she was developing.

"Hi, honey-bunny," she said as I entered the kitchen.

"Hey," I said, dumping my backpack onto the floor near the door.

She looked at me. "Everything okay?"

I sighed and sat down at the kitchen table. I didn't want to discuss Colin with my mom, so I started with my second-biggest concern. "I'm worried that the *Yay Gourmet* article will have mistakes."

She put her wooden spoon down on the spoon rest and turned to look at me. "Oh, sweetheart, don't worry. I'm sure it will be fine."

"Yes, but what if they get things really, really wrong? Like, what if they misquote us or give the wrong address for the store, or have the wrong description for one of our flavors and it makes our ice cream sound gross?"

My mom laughed, and wiping her hands on a dishtowel, she crossed the room to sit next to me at the table. "Allie! Remain calm! We just have to trust the reporter to get things right." She tapped the table thoughtfully. "Maybe we can ask them to check our quotes with us once the article is ready? But . . . at a certain point we just have to let go and trust that it will all come out okay. It usually does."

But I was shaking my head. "No. It seems that it usually *doesn't* come out all right. We just don't see the corrections when, or *if*, they run later. We must read things all the time that are wrong! And we don't even know it! It's like . . . how each person supposedly eats a pound of dirt in their life, or hundreds of bugs each year! The mistakes are just hidden, and they sneak by and we don't even realize it."

My mom took my hand and smoothed it, the way she did when I was sick. It always calmed me down. "What is it that Anne of Green Gables always says about enjoying things?" asked my mom. She knew that my favorite childhood books were the Anne of Green Gables series. That was why I'd named my cat Diana—after Anne's best friend.

I sighed. I knew what Mom was trying to do. Cheer me up by making me think of my favorite book.

My mom jiggled my hand and teased, "Come

on! I know you know the quote! What is it?"

"'It's been my experience . . . ,'" I muttered.

"Louder!" said my mom, laughing.

"'It's been my experience that you can nearly always enjoy things if . . .'" I trailed off.

"If what?" demanded my mom, shaking my hand from side to side.

"'It's been my experience that you can nearly always enjoy things if you make up your mind firmly that you will!'" I blurted in exasperation, but I was laughing now too. "Okay? Satisfied?"

My mom smiled. "Yes! Now come on, Allie. Stop borrowing trouble. Don't worry about things you can't control. Just prepare for the worst but plan for the best. Look on the bright side. It might be fun! And the article might turn out *better* than we even expect or hope!"

"How can you be such an optimist?" I grumbled.

"You have to be an optimist to be an entrepreneur, my dear. Otherwise, who would ever dare to start a business?"

"Okay, fine. But what about the photos? How are we going to make things look delicious? The ice cream will all melt!"

My mom pursed her lips. I'd stumped her with that one. "Well, they're the professionals. I'm sure they'll have some ideas," she said.

"Yeah, yeah!" I wanted to say, but I didn't.

CHAPTER FOUR
TO DO

That night at dinner my mom announced that she'd just received an e-mail setting the date for the *Yay Gourmet* interview.

"A week from this Sunday," she said happily.

"So twelve days," I added.

"Yup! And I'm going to need my best ice cream helpers there that day. Will you please check that Sierra and Tamiko will be there for sure?"

"Uh-huh," I agreed, twirling the spaghetti Bolognese on my fork.

"Great. You're my best employees, after all," said my mom.

I laughed. "You don't have that many to choose from!"

"Well, you're also my most photogenic," she added.

"Wait, we're going to be in the pictures?" I hadn't even considered that before.

"Yes. I mean, I would assume so," said my mom, shrugging.

"Me too?" asked my little brother, Tanner.

"Of course. You're my best customer!" said my mom.

Tanner wiggled happily in his seat and wiped his saucy cheek with his shirt.

"Tanner!" I cried. He had the most disgusting manners. "That is NOT the kind of thing you can do when the reporter and photographer are there!"

"What?" he asked.

"Ack!" I was so exasperated. Tanner had such bad manners, he didn't even *know* what he was doing wrong. I turned back to my mother. "Okay, Mom, so let me get this straight. We're going to help prepare the things to be photographed, so they need to look perfect and delicious. We're going to be *in* some of the photos, so we have to look awesome. They'll photograph the store, so it needs to look amazing, and we have to carefully plan what we will say, so

37

that they don't get anything wrong or misquote us in any way."

"Yes," said my mom, looking slightly less enthusiastic than before. "And I have firmly made up my mind to enjoy it."

"Right," I said, raising an eyebrow at her.

After dinner I raced upstairs to try another video chat with my besties. This time I got them.

"Hey, y'all!"

"Howdy!" said Sierra.

"What *up*," said Tamiko.

"The date is set for *Yay Gourmet*," I said flatly.

"Wait, are you not psyched anymore?" asked Sierra, her eyebrows knit in concern.

I sighed. "Well, the thing is, I've just realized this week how much can go wrong."

"Like what? The freezer breaks down?" Tamiko said, and then cackled.

"Don't joke!" I said.

"Well, what?" asked Sierra.

I listed my many concerns and sat there glumly while they considered them all.

"Hmm, you do have a point," admitted Sierra.

"Nah, stop worrying," said Tamiko. "We just have to be super-prepared, super-organized. We need to make a list!" she crowed. "Get a pen, writer-girl."

I grabbed a pen and some paper and sat there, poised to write down Tamiko's thoughts.

"Okay. In no particular order, here goes! We need outfits; we have to decide on a look for each of us. It should be edgy but not weird, or we'll turn people off. We need to consider your mom's outfit and incorporate that. What is she wearing? She'll need to get her hair and makeup done professionally. For our own hair, makeup, and clothing, I will be in charge, of course. The store needs to be cleaned from top to bottom that morning. We can do that. Get your mom to have the windows washed too. All the ice cream buckets need to be fresh and full in the freezer bins. Then we need to practice making the best-selling items this Sunday. What else? Read the list back to me."

My pen was flying over the paper. Now I stopped and read. "Our outfits. My mom's outfit. Hair and makeup. Clean store. Window washer. Full bins. Practice sundaes." I looked up. Tamiko was nodding.

"Good. Good start. What else?"

"What about a soundtrack?" I asked. Tamiko liked to "curate" our playlist for the store. My mom let her do it because she was good at it.

"Ooh! Wait, wait! I know! Can we have the Wild-flowers playing?" asked Sierra. "Pretty please?" She batted her long, dark eyelashes at us hopefully.

"Yeah, of course," said Tamiko, right as I said, "No!" forcefully.

They both stared at me like I'd lost my mind.

I shrugged. "I'm sorry, Sierra, but the last thing I need is for Colin's girlfriend to get discovered while my family's shop is being discovered."

"Colin and Tessa are going out?" blurted Tamiko.

"She didn't say anything to me at practice today!" Sierra was shocked.

"Well, I mean . . . I don't know if they're actually boyfriend-girlfriend. Yet," I added darkly.

"So he told you he liked her?" asked Tamiko.

"Not exactly," I admitted.

Sierra looked at me. "Well, what did he say about her?"

"Um, actually . . . nothing."

Tamiko let out a short burst of air. "So why are you calling them boyfriend and girlfriend, then?"

I took a deep breath in through my nose. "I don't know. Patrick said something at school about them. I just assumed . . ."

Sierra was shaking her head. "She would have said something, I'm sure. We all know she has a crush on him."

I cringed inside, just hearing those words.

"Okay. Let's deal with the soundtrack issue closer to the date," said Tamiko.

But after we hung up, Sierra texted me. Do you want me to ask Tessa if anything is going on?

I waited exactly zero seconds before replying NO! and hitting send.

Then I added, Thanks. And sent that, too.

Sierra did not reply.

I avoided Colin for the rest of the week. I knew it was chicken of me, but I couldn't face him. On Thursday night I gave myself a good talking-to. Did I like Colin? Yes. Did I like Colin as a crush? *Maybe.* Every time my brain tried to answer that question, it would just freeze. I mean, I wasn't ready to be dating, like boyfriend-girlfriend. I just didn't want anyone *else* to date him. It sounded sort of crazy when I laid it all out like that, but what could I do? Anyway, it wasn't up to me. I was pretty sure that by the end of that weekend I'd hear that Colin and Tessa were a couple.

On Sunday morning Tamiko and Sierra met at my house well before we were due at work. Tamiko had brought a phone full of selfies of her in six different outfits, from every possible angle. (She'd used a tripod.) Sierra had an armload of outfits to try on, and she and Tamiko were set to attack my closet and my mom's closet to arrange our outfits for the interview. Tamiko wanted a very basic theme—everything kind of had to go together, but not matchy-matchy like uniforms. One of her ideas was "cornucopia," which meant "horn of plenty." She wanted a look of "abundance," so she wanted us all in splashy florals and bright colors. I had a Hawaiian-print dress I could wear for that theme, and my mom had a jazzy blouse with hot-pink cabbage roses all over it. Tamiko and Sierra each had bright floral looks that could go along with it too.

Another theme Tamiko liked was "1980s retro," which she said was trending right now. That meant black with pastels, or very bright solid colors contrasting with each other (like a hot-yellow shirt with electric-blue pants). I wasn't as crazy about that theme because I didn't think it went well with the look of Molly's. Molly's was all cream and pale blue and gold—kind of classic and old-fashioned-looking.

Tamiko's simplest theme was "disappear into the background," which consisted of our most neutral clothes—anything in beige, cream, or gray. She said we'd look like ice cream scientists and that the ice cream and sundaes would stand out, with us as a pale backdrop. This made the most sense to me but was the least fun. We decided to let my mom decide.

Downstairs my mom was doing her books, which meant balancing all her accounts—the money coming in and the money going out. She was happy for a quick break.

"Hi, girls. Oh, Allie, don't you look pretty in that dress!" I was still wearing the Hawaiian-print dress. My friends and I exchanged smiles.

"That's what we're here to ask you," I said. "We wanted to know what you're thinking in terms of outfits for the *Yay Gourmet* interview next Sunday."

She lifted her reading glasses onto her head and put down her pen, then leaned back in her chair, folding her arms. "Hmmm. I hadn't even given it a moment's thought. What do *you* girls think?"

"Well, we had a few different ideas . . . ," I began, and then Tamiko took over. She could discuss this stuff for hours, so I was happy to have her take the lead. She flipped through her phone, showing my mom her ideas, and my mom smiled and nodded as she looked.

After the mini fashion show, my mom was impressed, I could tell.

"Thank you all for taking this so seriously! It could be a really big break for Molly's, and I am so grateful to you girls for realizing that."

Tamiko and Sierra beamed, and I felt really good.

"I personally think the bright, happy colors and patterns are the most fun," Mom said. "What did you call it? Cornucopia?"

Tamiko nodded.

"I think we should go with that. Why not have everything pretty and colorful, right?"

"Great!" I said. That was my favorite look, anyway.

"We had a few other thoughts," said Tamiko, glancing at me to see if it was okay to read our to-do list to my mom. I nodded, and she worked her way through the list.

My mom was nodding along. "Great point about the window washer. I'll call them tomorrow." She made a note on her pad. "For the hair and makeup, I'll get my friend Annie from the Salon on the Square to come over that morning and help us out."

"All of us?" I said in surprise.

"Sure. Why not? It will be fun!" said my mom. "If everyone can just arrive with wet hair, it will go faster. I'll get a time from Annie and let you know."

My friends and I exchanged smiles again. This might be fun after all!

"Another thing we have to work out is which flavors are being showcased, and what specialties we should make for the reporter and photographer," Tamiko said.

"Yes, great point," my mom replied. "Maybe . . . Could you girls work on that while I finish the accounts here? Then we can discuss it at work today?"

"Yup!" I said.

My friends and I left my mom to her work and went back to my room to create a sample menu. The first thing I did was show them the food photography book.

"Yummy!" said Tamiko, looking at the sundae

45

on the cover. "Not too imaginative, but a good, basic-looking traditional hot fudge sundae."

"Yeah, but check this out," I said. I took the book from Tamiko and opened to a bookmark I'd left in the ice cream chapter. Then I handed the book back to her, and Tamiko was silent as she pored over the pages.

"Hmmm. Okay. Wow. Gross!" She looked up at me. "This sounds disgusting."

"I know," I said.

"What is it?" asked Sierra.

I explained about the lard and the glue and the paint and all the other tricks of the trade. Sierra was grossed out too.

"Well, we can't do all that!" said Tamiko. "Maybe one or two things, but not the lard or whatever."

"I know," I agreed glumly. "But it's going to look bad."

"Not necessarily. *Yay Gourmet* seems to like a messy, natural look. See?"

Tamiko pulled up the website on her phone and scrolled through some photos. "These look delish," she said.

I looked at the phone over her shoulder. "Yeah,

but that could be glue, and that might have been shellacked, and that might be brown paint." I pointed out a variety of details.

Tamiko sagged a little on my bed. "I see what you mean. Well, you know what we have to do—work really hard today on practicing making sundaes that are beautiful."

"Yeah. And hope the photographer knows what they're doing," added Sierra.

Tamiko nodded and reached out for a fist bump.

Sierra said, "It's funny how your mom doesn't seem nervous about this at all. Are we overreacting?"

I shook my head. "No. I think she's underreacting."

Tamiko laughed and patted my shoulder. "Don't worry, Ali-li. Miko is here now, and everything will be just fine."

"So what should we do for our featured flavors?" I asked.

Tamiko pulled out her notebook. "Let's look back at the taste test we did a while ago." She flipped from page to page; then she found it. "Aha! Okay. Here we go. We decided our best flavor is Banana Pudding."

"Mmm. I love the Banana Pudding!" I agreed dreamily.

"I wonder how it will look in photos, though. I mean, it doesn't have a lot of 'curb appeal,' as they say on those real estate TV shows," said Sierra.

"I know what you mean. The goodness is invisible to the naked eye!" said Tamiko, wiggling her eyebrows up and down.

"What were the runners-up?" I asked Tamiko, peeking at the book over her shoulder.

The list said:

- Kitchen Sink (vanilla ice cream with crumbled pretzels and potato chips)
- Hokey Pokey (with bits of honeycomb toffee)
- Strawberry Shortcake
- Banana Pudding
- Lavender Blackberry
- Chocolate Mint Chip
- Peppermint
- Candy Bar
- Lime Sorbet
- Balsamic Strawberry
- Butterscotch Chocolate Chunk
- Rocky Road
- Saint Louis Cake
- Vanilla

- Chocolate
- Lemon Blueberry
- Cereal Milk
- Cinnamon (with crumbled lace butter cookies in it)

"Hmmmm," said Tamiko, scanning the list. "Which are the most photogenic flavors?"

Sierra leaned in for a look. "Hey! I don't see my favorite in there!"

Tamiko laughed. "Which is your favorite today, Sierra?"

Sierra was always changing her mind.

"Cookies and Cream!"

Tamiko tapped her foot on the floor as she thought. Then she said, "You know, this list wasn't the list of all the flavors that Molly's sells. It was just that week's flavors. We need to create a master list and work from that."

Quickly we added about twenty more flavors that we could remember, including Cookies and Cream. I popped downstairs to show it to my mom, and she agreed that we had it all. Back upstairs, we began debating which flavors to showcase.

"First of all," Tamiko started, "we should print up

the list of flavors on a really nice document and give it to the reporter for reference. Maybe they can run it as a sidebar to the piece."

I was nodding before Tamiko had even finished explaining her idea.

"Brilliant," I said.

"Then let's think about what would look good in photos and taste good. Also, we need some variety. Like, it can't all be chocolaty flavors," said Tamiko.

We debated back and forth for a while. Sierra was really fixated on taste, but then I said, "Look, the reporter can sample anything he or she wants. It's just what we're going to feature and prepare for the photos." That loosened things up, and we all rapidly agreed on three flavors to showcase: Lime Sorbet, Rockin' Rocky Road, and, of course, Banana Pudding . . . but in a unicorn sundae (which was an invention of Tamiko's and was the house specialty).

"One chocolaty flavor, one fruity flavor, and one over-the-top sundae. Perfect!" said Sierra.

With that decided, we all looked at one another and grinned. Then Tamiko high-fived me and Sierra. I breathed a sigh of relief.

"Thanks for helping, you guys. It means a lot to me. And my mom, too, of course."

"We care about Molly's just as much as you do!" said Tamiko.

"You guys are the best!" My heart was warmed by my friends' enthusiasm. Maybe this would all work out okay.

CHAPTER FIVE
SCOOP PERFECTION

We were slammed again at work that afternoon, but in a good way. With the weather heating up, people were thinking about ice cream more than ever. It was exhilarating to handle a rush. My besties and I—the Sprinkle Sundays sisters—handled it all with grace, but I still worried about the following week.

"What if we drop a sundae next week while the reporter's here?" I whispered to Tamiko as she handed a loaded bowl of ice cream and toppings over the counter to a customer.

"Okay, now you're just being a worrywart," scolded Tamiko. "Dropping a sundae is not news-worthy. They will *not* cover that in the story, I can guarantee you."

I took a deep breath in through my nose and smiled for the next customer.

When things quieted down during the pre-dinner lull, we started practicing our sample scoops and sundaes.

"Okay, so I researched perfect ice cream scoops online . . . ," began Tamiko.

Sierra and I exchanged grins.

"Of course she did!" said Sierra.

"Laugh all you want. I'll just keep my pro scooping advice to myself!" huffed Tamiko.

"Just kidding, *chica*!" said Sierra. "Tell us."

Tamiko was, of course, dying to tell us what to do. It didn't take any more prodding to get her to do it.

"The trick, as you know, is a very hot scooper. Soak it in the hot water bin or run it under hot water for a minute."

"Right," I said. We already knew that.

"Also, it's best if you store the ice cream very, very, very cold."

"Uh-huh," I agreed.

"Check," said Sierra, peeping at our freezer thermostat setting.

"And it's best if you take out the ice cream a few minutes before you scoop it," said Tamiko.

I shook my head. "We can't do that. It's against the health code. Also, it ruins the ice cream—all that melting and refreezing."

"Right. But here's the most important tip—something I'd never heard before, and it works like a charm. When you put your scoop into the ice cream, you want to carve out the ice cream in an S curve, like this, see?"

Instead of the normal straight-down-and-out scoop (shaped like a big letter *C* going down), Tamiko reached down to the bucket of Rockin' Rocky Road and curved the scooper to the left and then the right, creating a giant S-shaped trough in the ice cream's surface.

Then she released the scoop onto a cone with a flick of her thumb against the lever and pressed it into place.

"Ta-da!" she said, holding the cone aloft in triumph.

"Wow! That really does work!" I said.

Sierra walked around the cone and admired it from every angle. It was a perfect, dense ball of brown-and-white ice cream. "Good job, Miko! It looks amazing!"

Tamiko smiled. "I know. That's how you guys need to do it."

Sierra and I each gave it a try (well, it took me two tries because I didn't dig deep enough at the start), and our scoops came out great.

"We should do this all the time!" said Sierra.

"Hmm. Careful," I cautioned. "A super-dense scoop of ice cream might be giving away more ice cream than we really want to each time."

Tamiko raised her eyebrows at me and wiggled them. "Are you trying to rip off our customers?"

"No, but you know what I mean. It's the same way that we don't want the scoops to be too giant. The profit is in the details here. Plus, we don't have time to make a perfect scoop every time, especially when we're busy. That's all."

Tamiko pushed her hair off her face and sighed. "True. Sometimes I wish we had one of those soft-serve ice cream machines in here. Wouldn't it be so much fun to squirt those wiggly ice creams into cones?"

"Yes! Totally," agreed Sierra.

"Soft serve is huge in Japan," said Tamiko. "They call it 'soft cream,' and they sell all these cool local flavors too. Just think of what your mom could come up with, Allie."

"I know. It would be fun to have one. We should research it."

"When I go to Japan this summer, I'll do some research. I think it could be amazing for sundaes, too. Hey, Allie, have you firmed up any plans for summer yet?" she asked.

"No, not yet. I haven't really had time. . . ." I wasn't sure how to negotiate a plan between my parents, now that they were divorced. It would be best if I could talk with them at the same time about it, but it always seemed to be a rush when they were together these days. I didn't want to speak to them separately and get separate answers and then have to be the go-between. I sighed. I hated not having a plan.

"Don't worry," said Sierra, patting my back and then pushing her hair off her forehead. "You'll find something cool to do."

"I hope it's cool!" I said. "Because it gets so hot here in the summer!"

We laughed, and Tamiko began to get us organized for sorbet scooping, which was a little different from ice cream scooping.

Tamiko had to readjust her ponytail before she leaned into the case, and it made me glad that I had on my polka-dot headband . . . the one Colin had admired the other day. It seemed like a million years had passed since then.

"Guys! I just thought of something!" I said. "We should all wear headbands for the shoot!"

"Cute idea!" agreed Sierra.

"Yeah," said Tamiko, coming up out of the case with her hair hanging in her eyes. "And more sanitary, too."

"I'll get some to match our colorful outfits," I offered.

"Great."

Tamiko pressed the scoop of sorbet into a cone, and it looked a little ragged.

"Hmm," I said, evaluating it.

"Not as pretty," said Sierra.

Tamiko sighed. "Trying again."

She dumped the first scoopful back into the tub and pressed it down, then re-scooped. She deposited the second scoop, and . . . it was still kind of lame-looking. The edges were ragged, and the scoop was a little chunky.

We all looked at it critically.

"If we could just smooth this part out . . . ," said Tamiko, carving at a side of the sorbet ball.

"Yeah, and even out that other ragged area where it's breaking apart," said Sierra, gesturing at the other side of the scoop.

"Maybe we should premake the scoops? Freeze them on a cookie sheet?" I suggested.

They turned to look at me.

"Genius!" cried Sierra.

"Love it, sistah!" said Tamiko.

Tamiko set about making a few perfect Lime Sorbet scoops by rolling them into dense snowballs while I got a cookie sheet and lined it with parchment paper. Soon Tamiko had four perfect scoops arrayed in a grid on the paper. She stowed it in the massive Deepfreeze in the back, and we'd check on it later to see how the scoops had held up.

We helped a family who came in, and then we turned to our final challenge: the perfect unicorn sundae.

"Okay, we want colors that pop!" said Tamiko forcefully.

"Pop!" echoed Sierra, clapping her hands.

"And contrasts that sizzle!" cheered Tamiko.

"Sizzle!" cried Sierra.

"And height, volume, and sparkle!" shouted Tamiko.

"Sparkle!" yelled Sierra.

By now we were all really laughing hard.

My mom came out from the back. "What's so funny up here?" she asked with a smile, ready to join our laughter.

"Just Tamiko and Sierra," I said, shaking my head and catching my breath.

"What are you girls working on?" she asked, surveying the scene.

"Trying to perfect the unicorn sundae for next weekend," I said.

"Aha! A noble and worthwhile pastime! But, girls, don't you have homework? I know you've stayed overtime today to do this, but I don't want it getting in the way of your more important commitments," she said.

"Nothing's more important than Molly's Ice Cream shop!" said Sierra enthusiastically.

"What she said!" said Tamiko, jerking a thumb toward Sierra.

My mom smiled. "I'm grateful that you feel that way, but your parents and teachers might not. I think you should call it a night."

"We will, Mom, right after we make this sundae!" I said.

"Okay. Dad's coming in ten minutes to pick you up, though."

"Okay, no time to waste!" I said to my friends.

Tamiko peered through the glass of the ice cream freezer. "Strawberry?"

"Sure!" I agreed.

"Or chocolate?" offered Sierra, a chocolate addict.

Tamiko looked at us wickedly. "One of each!"

She scooped and rinsed, then repeated. The brown and hot-pink scoops looked amazing next to each other in the long oval-shaped bowl. Tamiko layered on the toppings: hot fudge, caramel, marshmallow, and a "sprinkle of happy." Then she plunged a swirly "unicorn horn" lollipop into one end of the sundae.

"Ta-da!" she said.

"Beautiful," sighed Sierra.

But I wasn't sure. I looked at it on the counter. Then I turned it in all directions. "We'll just need to make sure the sauce puddles evenly in the bowl," I said. "And . . . let's make sure you put the hot toppings out in little cups before you add them to the ice cream. They need to cool off a bit before you put them on top. See how it melts the ice cream into puddles when it comes in contact with it? It's too hot to look pretty."

Tamiko's eyebrows were raised high, and she was looking at me skeptically with her arms folded across her chest.

"Okay?" I said.

"Sure. That's fine, Allie. Just . . ." She glanced at Sierra, who was avoiding looking at her.

"Just what?" I asked.

"Just . . . chill," she said.

"Look, someone has to make sure this all works out," I said.

"Isn't that kind of your mom's role?" asked Sierra quietly.

"I guess, but she doesn't seem worried enough to me!" I said, my irritation flaring.

My friends shared a look.

"Listen, Allie—" began Tamiko.

But just then my dad and Tanner walked in. "Hello, ice cream ladies!" said my dad cheerfully.

"Hey, Mr. Shear!" my friends chimed. All my friends liked my dad. He was good about being interested in us and then leaving us alone.

"Wow! Look at that sundae!" said my dad. "What a beauty!"

Tamiko glared at me meaningfully. I shrugged.

"Can we get ice cream, Dad?" asked Tanner, tugging on my dad's shirt.

"We can get some to go. Why don't each of you pick a flavor and we'll take home a pint of each? Okay, buddy?"

Tanner nodded.

"I'm going to go chat with your mom," said my dad, and he headed into the back. I watched him go. This would be a good time to discuss camp with both of them present. My friends were chatting with Tanner, and he was giggling as he chose his flavor.

"Sierra, could you please make a Rockin' Rocky Road pint for me? I'll be right back," I said, and Sierra agreed.

I went backstage, as we called the back of the

shop, and I could hear my parents' voices. Like always, I automatically checked to see if there was stress or anger in their tones. With all the fighting in our house when I was growing up, you had to know how to time things. Like, sometimes you just had to make yourself invisible and go hide in a book.

But right now it seemed calm. (Most of the time since they'd split up, it had seemed calm, which was nice. Better.)

"Hey, guys," I said by way of announcing myself.

"Hi, honey," said my dad. "Are you guys ready?"

"Almost." I leaned in the doorway of my mom's office.

"What's up?" asked my mom.

"Um, I was just wondering . . ." I picked at a cuticle that had ripped. I almost didn't want to ask about camp because it was better to not know for sure and think I still might be going than to know for sure that I wasn't. "What are you thinking for me for this summer?" I said it all in a rush, like ripping off a Band-Aid.

My dad's eyebrows shot up in surprise, and he looked at my mom. Her mouth had dropped open. "Oh my gosh." She found her voice first. "I haven't even focused on summer yet!"

"Yeah," I said, shrugging. "It's coming up."

"Were you thinking about going back to Holly Oaks again this summer?" asked my dad, referring to my camp up north.

I tried to read their expressions. I didn't want to say yes, only to find that there was no way they could afford it or spare me. But I didn't want to say no and risk not going if they could make it work.

"I don't know," I said.

"Have you thought about doing anything else?" asked my dad.

"Not really." I shook my head.

"Do you feel like you've outgrown camp?" asked my mom, studying my face.

"Yes and no," I said truthfully.

My parents looked at each other, then back at me. "Why don't we discuss it tonight?" offered my dad. He looked at my mom, and she nodded.

"Good idea. Let me know what you two decide," she said.

"We'd better get going," said my dad as he turned to leave.

My mom followed us out to say good-bye to Tanner and send my friends home.

"Psyched for next week, Mrs. S.!" said Tamiko as she put her apron into the laundry bin.

"*Yay Gourmet!*" cheered Sierra.

My mom laughed. "Thanks, girls! Looking forward to it!"

Outside, Tamiko's dad was waiting to drive them home. I waved at their car until they turned a corner and I couldn't see them anymore. I loved spending time with my Sprinkle Sundays sisters, but the time always went by so quickly. I missed them already.

CHAPTER SIX
THE CUTE COUPLE

After we returned to my dad's apartment and ate dinner, my dad insisted that we take a walk. We went on a walk almost every time Tanner and I visited. The air felt refreshing, but I didn't like how my dad was trying so hard to make it a new "family tradition." It just reminded me of all the family traditions we had lost since my parents had split up.

"So, Allie, tell me what you're thinking for summer," said my dad.

It was easier to talk with him when I didn't have to look right at him. I sighed and watched an airplane cross the sky. Did I want to go all the way up to New Hampshire again for the summer? Suddenly it seemed like a huge effort.

"I don't know. I love camp. I love the weather and the people and all the traditions. But . . . maybe I'm getting a little too old for it. And maybe . . . Mom needs me here, like, to watch Tanner and stuff."

"Hmm," said my dad. "I wouldn't worry about what Mom needs. What do you *want*?" he asked.

"I think it would be fun to maybe do a few different things," I said, suddenly realizing as I said it that this was true.

"Does the camp have a half session? Like, three weeks instead of seven?" my dad asked.

"Yes!" I said, looking at him. "It does. I could do that!" I said. Why hadn't *I* thought of that?

He smiled. "Okay! And then when you get back, you'd just need to find something to do the rest of the time."

"I could babysit Tanner and work at the store," I said.

He nodded. "But I'd like to see you do something in addition to that. I'd like you to get a little more out of the summer. Maybe there's a local camp you could go to?"

I scrunched my nose. "I'm a little old for day camp," I said.

"I'm not!" piped Tanner. I hadn't realized he'd been listening.

My dad laughed. "That's right, bud! And I think you should go to that awesome one again that you liked last summer."

"Cool," said Tanner.

The sky was beginning to turn orange and pink. "Let's go home," my dad said, then turned to me. "Why don't you look around town and see if there's a fun camp or program you could do, okay, honey?"

"Okay," I said. "And I'll get the info on the half session for camp." I felt a huge relief and sense of excitement at having at least part of my summer in place.

"Perfect. And I'll organize it all with Mom," said my dad.

"Thanks, Dad," I said, hugging him.

As we turned back to the apartment, something caught my eye up ahead. There were two people walking about half a block in front of us, a boy and a girl about my age. The boy had a black backpack with a neon yellow lightning bolt down the back, just like . . . Colin's. And the girl was carrying a guitar.

My heart sank. It was Colin and Tessa, and this

was the only way back to my dad's from here without going blocks out of the way. We'd have to pass right by them.

Millions of questions swirled through my mind. What was Colin doing here on this street? Why was he with Tessa, just the two of them? How did they know each other, anyway? What were they talking about so excitedly? Colin was gesturing with his hands as he spoke, and Tessa was laughing. I felt sick.

"Right, Allie?" My father and Tanner had been chatting while I'd been watching Colin and Tessa. I hadn't even been listening, I was so focused on the scene ahead of us.

"Huh?" I asked, clueless about the conversation.

Colin and Tessa stopped abruptly at the bus stop just as we drew near. When he turned to look for the bus, Colin spotted me.

"Allie! What are you doing here?" he called.

My heart sank. I closed the distance between us in a few slow steps. "Hey, Colin," I said.

"Hi, kids," said my dad.

"Um, Dad, this is Colin from school." I introduced them, and they shook hands and exchanged pleasantries. "And this is my brother, Tanner." I looked over at Tanner, who was calmly picking his nose as he watched a kid go by on a skateboard.

"Tanner!" I scolded. Colin laughed, and my face grew red.

"Allie, you know Tessa, right? From the Wildflowers? At Patrick's party?"

"Hi," I said. I felt so nervous! What was wrong with me?

She smiled. "Hi, Allie. I'm friends with Sierra." Tessa actually seemed really nice and friendly, and under other circumstances, I might have liked her. Right then I just nodded. She was dressed in a cute sports outfit, but her hair looked nice and she had on little earrings. I felt like a slob in my messy ponytail and grubby work clothes.

There was an awkward pause.

"Allie's mom is the owner of Molly's," said Colin to Tessa.

"I love that place!" Tessa's eyes lit up. "I've only been there once so far, but the Cereal Milk flavor is amazing!"

"No way!" Colin cried. "That's my favorite flavor too."

"I *knew* it would be your favorite too. Great minds

70

think alike!" Tessa said, and they high-fived.

I wanted to throw up. They seemed like really good friends—like, the kind of friends I considered Colin and me to be. But suddenly Patrick's words from class echoed in my head: "a cute couple." They *were* a cute couple, not just friends. I could see it from a mile away!

And here I'd known Colin for months now and had no idea what his favorite ice cream flavor was. In fact, there was a ton I didn't know about him. I watched Tessa and Colin joke about ice cream and couldn't think of anything else to say. I felt invisible.

"Well, I guess we'd better get home before the sun sets," said my dad. I loved him so much right then.

Mumbling a quick good-bye, I turned away from the couple.

"Bye, Allie! See you tomorrow!" called Colin.

I waved and walked on.

A few paces out of their earshot, my dad said, "They seem nice."

I shrugged.

"That's Allie's boyfriend!" said Tanner.

My dad looked at me in surprise. I wanted the

ground to open up and swallow Tanner right then, or me. Either one.

"He's not my boyfriend," I snarled.

Tanner looked at me in doubt and then looked at my dad and shrugged.

My dad was watching me.

"What?" I asked grumpily.

"Nothing!" said my dad, all innocent. "He seemed like a nice kid. It makes me happy to see you with new friends who are nice."

"He's not a friend," I said. "Just someone from school."

Because that was how I was sure he thought of me—as just someone from school.

Before I went to bed that night, I thought about telling Sierra and Tamiko what had happened. It all felt too complicated to explain, though. Instead I texted my besties in our group chat:

Just remembered. We should all do our nails before the Yay Gourmet interview. Our hands should look good in case they're in the photos. Not grubby. Okay?

Okay! Sierra replied.

K, said Tamiko.

I replied with the kissy-face emoji and Thx.

Luckily I didn't have to ride the bus for the next four days because I was staying at my dad's and he drove me to school. I saw Colin at school from afar and in the class we shared, but I didn't need to speak to him. He always looked at me expectantly with a smile, like he wanted to chat, but I turned away. All I could think of now was him with Tessa, and I felt like I didn't know how to talk to him anymore.

I was nervous about running into him at lunch, so I took to my old habit of heading to the library during my lunch break. Mrs. K. was happy to see me and always had a stack of things for me to do—books to shelve, themed displays to set up, the usual. I sometimes thought she kind of made up jobs for me, but I didn't mind. I loved being there with all the books and readers and chatting with her. It seemed like she'd read everything in the library.

After my chores were finished, I kept finding myself pulled to the food magazines in the periodical section. I'd sit and read descriptions of techniques and fancy foods, and even though I'd already eaten my sandwich, my mouth would water. I couldn't help but wonder, as I read the articles, had the reporter really gotten the information right? Were there errors that I didn't notice? And how had they gotten the food to look so good? With a critical eye, I tried to discern the use of lard or glue or paint, but I couldn't.

By the fourth day, Mrs. K. commented on my "fascination with food writing."

"I'd like to direct you to some good food writing, mm–hmm," she said. "I can see how much you love it."

"Oh!" I said in surprise. "It's not that I love it. . . ." How could I phrase it without sounding nuts? "I'm just . . . My mom has a reporter coming to her ice cream store this weekend to write an article, and I'm . . . nervous about how it's going to go. I'm just trying to see what could go wrong so that maybe we can avoid it. I want to be prepared."

Mrs. K.'s eyebrows knit together in concern. "What *could* go wrong?"

I sighed heavily. "Lots of things! They could misquote us, get the facts wrong, dislike the ice cream, make my mom out to be inexperienced, laugh at us—"

74

"But why would they do that?"

I shrugged. "I don't know. Maybe because the business is new and we don't really know what we're doing?"

"I see. Hmm. Honestly, though, that's difficult to imagine. I don't think people would do that."

"Well, we might drop an ice cream or make a mess or something."

"Umm, hmm. I don't think people would be that mean-spirited in ice cream reporting." Mrs. K. nodded and busied herself restacking some books on her cart. "Are you well prepared for the interview?" she asked.

I took a deep breath. "I am. And I *think* my friends are. But I'm not so sure about my mom. She seems to think everything's going to be just fine!"

Mrs. K. looked at me. "I'm sure she's right. Here. I found what I was looking for. M.F.K. Fisher. Food writing. A classic. Give this book a try, okay, hmmm?" She put a book into my hands. It was kind of old and beat-up and did not have an interesting cover at all. It looked like it belonged in a thrift shop.

"Thanks," I said. I stowed it in my book bag and headed out.

As I trudged up the stairs to class, I thought of a couple more things I needed to remind my friends about for Sunday. I group-texted them:

Guys: we should all do face masks Saturday night so our skin looks amazing, in case we're in the photos, ok?

Tamiko replied, OK.

Sierra didn't reply.

When school was over, I went straight to Molly's to see my mom. I hadn't seen her in four days, and I missed her, but I also wanted to make sure everything was on track for the *Yay Gourmet* interview and photo shoot.

At Molly's my mom was behind the counter, and it was quiet.

"Hi, sweetheart!" she said, excited to see me. I went behind the counter for a hug, and we caught up. "Dad told me about your summer planning chat," she said.

I was surprised. I always forgot that my parents might be interacting without me and Tanner around—like on the phone or something.

"What do you think?" I asked.

"Brilliant. I agree totally. I've already contacted

Holly Oaks, and if you give me the green light, I'll send in the deposit."

"Can we afford it?" I asked my mom.

"Absolutely," she said. "The full summer tuition might have been a little much for us this year, but I love the three-week idea."

"Thanks," I said with a sigh of relief.

"Can you research some ideas for the rest of your summer?"

"Okay, but how?"

My mom squinted as she thought. "Maybe your school library or the guidance counselor would keep a file of local stuff?"

I smiled as I thought of Mrs. K. "Great. I know who to ask." I looked around the store. "Are you all set for the interview?" I asked.

My mom nodded. "The window washers and the cleaners are coming early Sunday before we open. I have all our prettiest flavors in the Deepfreeze, ready to go. I have my outfit that you girls picked out, all ironed and ready. I think we should be fine!"

"Okay." I breathed in deeply. "Okay."

"Don't worry, sweetheart. It will be all right. *Yay Gourmet* isn't out to ruin us, you know!" She laughed.

I raised my eyebrows. "I hope not."

"Listen, can you stay for a few minutes? I just want to pop out to the grocery store and pick up something for dinner."

"Sure, no problem," I agreed. I put my hair into a ponytail, washed my hands, and donned an apron.

It was quiet, but I couldn't really get into spreading out my homework on a café table, in case someone came in. I opened my backpack and spotted the book Mrs. K. had lent me. Sighing, I decided to flip through it.

Within minutes, I was totally engrossed.

This writer, M.F.K. Fisher, was old-fashioned, and I didn't understand a lot of it, but I liked the way she described food.

The door jingled as someone came in, and I had to wrench my attention away from the book and refocus on the store. It was a group of kids my age, which I normally didn't mind if my friends were with me working. But today I was alone, so I felt exposed and awkward.

The kids were nice, though. I didn't recognize any of them except the final kid—Daniel from the school paper staff. He'd been in the meeting the other day, when I'd blurted my dumb idea about reprinting the *Yay Gourmet* article.

"Hi!" I said brightly, with a smile.

"Hi. Could I please have a peanut butter milkshake?" he asked.

"Sure!" I smiled again, waiting for him to say something about school or the paper, but he just looked at me blankly. Suddenly I realized that he didn't recognize me.

My face turned red as I began to scoop the ice cream. *How mortifying to be so unmemorable*, I thought. *Maybe if I were cooler, like Tessa, people would remember me.* I set the milkshake on the stand to mix and rang up the other kids who were waiting. Then I returned to Daniel's shake, poured it out, and told him the price. I didn't add a sprinkle of happy. It was my own private rebellion.

Daniel handed me the money and said thanks— totally polite but still having no idea who I was—and then they all sat down at one of the tables, scraping the chairs over to make one big group.

I washed the scoopers, wiped up stray sprinkles and spilled sauce, and half listened to them chat. Then I heard the name "Colin," and my ears perked up.

"He's the assistant editor of our paper," said Daniel.

I strained to hear what the other kid was saying, and I could have sworn I heard the name "Tessa." My heart dropped. I hoped people weren't mentioning them together!

But then Daniel distinctly said, "No. Not her. They're not a couple."

And where only minutes before, I had been unhappy with Daniel, now I was totally grateful to him! I wanted to run out from behind the counter with his sprinkle of happy after all! But what else was he saying?

". . . someone else."

Darn it! I couldn't hear. Something about someone else?

The subject changed, and the kids began talking about sports, and the moment was gone, but I was dying to know what the deal was with Colin and Tessa. Were they not a couple? Was Colin interested in someone else? Ugh. I needed to know! The kids all finished their ice creams and left without my ever hearing more about Colin.

Shortly thereafter my mom returned and sent me home to do my homework, handing me twenty dollars for covering her shift. I tried to refuse it, but she insisted.

"If you don't take it, I won't feel like I can ask you for help again!" she said with a smile.

"Thanks, Mom."

As I bent to put it into my wallet inside my backpack, she spotted the book Mrs. K. had given me. "Ooh! M.F.K. Fisher! We read her writing in college! Do you like it?"

I nodded. "The librarian at school gave it to me because I've been reading all the food magazines. She said it's a classic. It's hard, but I do like it."

My mom nodded. "A little out-of-date, too. But if you like food writing, I'd love to go to the library in town with you and take out some books. There are so many great ones!"

"Okay. Thanks!" I agreed. "Next week."

"It's a date!" she agreed.

As I walked home, Tamiko and Allie called me from Tamiko's mom's car on speakerphone.

"Hey, Ali-li!" said Tamiko.

"Hi, Miko!"

"I'm here too!" said Sierra.

"What's up, girls?" I asked.

"Want to go to dinner at the crêpe place tomorrow?" asked Sierra. "Tamiko's mom just offered to take us because she has to run an errand over there."

"Yes! Definitely! I'm in."

"Perfect. We'll pick you up at five thirty."

"Thanks! Bye!" I felt warm and happy. I loved having weekend plans with my besties to look forward to, even if I did have to get though a bus ride with Colin in between.

Later I remembered a few more details for the interview and shoot on Sunday, and I group-texted my besties.

Flowers for Sunday? What do u think? Also, shld I pick up paper straws? Plastic straws very bad for environment, even tho we have a lot of stock to get thru.

No one replied.

CHAPTER SEVEN
A NIGHT IN FRANCE

The next morning I had butterflies in my stomach, dreading seeing Colin on the bus. I half wanted him to be there and I half didn't. I missed him, friend or crush, whichever it was. I wasn't sure. But the Tessa thing was still swirling in my mind, whether Daniel was right or not. *Better if Colin's not on the bus*, I decided.

And then, sure enough, he *was* on the bus, sitting in our usual spot. He started waving as soon as I climbed aboard. I looked all around, hoping for some sort of diversion, someone calling me to sit with them instead, but there wasn't anyone. It was undeniable: Colin was my best friend at school, and there was no way to avoid him. I'd have to go back there and sit with him.

"Hey, mystery lady!" he said as I drew close. "Where have you been the past week? I thought you'd suddenly gotten four years older, gotten your license, and given up the bus!"

At least he's noticed, I thought as I swung into the seat. I shrugged, trying to maintain the air of mystery. "I've been around," I said. "At my dad's, actually."

He looked at me carefully. Then he said, "Well, I've missed you."

Suddenly I was grinning at him like a fool, and I had to turn and look out the window because my cheeks hurt.

"What's new?" he asked.

I shrugged and turned back, my smile under control now. "Oh, the usual . . ." And then we were off and chatting, back to normal. There was always so much for us to talk about! We talked about the school paper (I did *not* mention the *Yay Gourmet* article again, thank you very much), and he talked about our English test. Then I told him about M.F.K. Fisher and my camp plans for the summer.

Suddenly there was a commotion ahead of us, and an overpowering sweet smell filled the bus. Then the Mean Team started.

"Palmerrrrrr!" Maria wailed. "You broke my brand-new perfume bottle!"

Colin and I looked at each other. We both grinned.

"SORRY!" Palmer cried. "I didn't know it would be so fragile!"

"Ugh, now I'm going to smell like *your* perfume instead of *my* perfume!" complained Blair.

Colin and I grimaced at the Mean Team's drama, and Colin turned to open the bus window to let the smell out.

"I really don't like the smell of flowers. It makes my allergies go haywire," he said quietly. "Last year I had to sit next to Palmer in math class. Her perfume was so strong that I finally couldn't stand it and asked the teacher to switch my seat."

"Wow," I said, making a mental note to never wear perfume around Colin (not that I wore perfume in the first place).

Then he grinned. "I've never told anyone about that besides you. Don't go spreading it around!"

I mimed zipping my mouth and throwing away the key, but inside I felt warm and fuzzy. *Never told anyone? Not even Tessa?* I knew I shouldn't have been comparing myself to Tessa, but it *did* feel good to have Colin sharing secrets with me. Suddenly I pictured him and Tessa high-fiving over Cereal Milk ice cream, and I cringed a little inside. *Don't get too possessive, Allie,* I cautioned myself.

I took a deep breath as the bus came to a stop outside school.

"What's up for the weekend?" Colin asked me as we inched our way down the bus aisle.

"Out tonight with friends, homework tomorrow and babysitting my brother, then work on Sunday. The reporter from the food website I mentioned is coming for the interview on Sunday." I couldn't help myself. I had to tell him!

"No way! That's awesome. Are you open to the public while they're there?"

"Yeah, I think so. For most of it anyway."

"Then I'd better come by with some friends and make sure the reporter knows that Molly's is super popular!"

I laughed. "Thanks!" I said. Then I realized that "friends" might mean Tessa, and my smile faded.

"See you then!" he said as we parted.

"See you," I managed to respond.

At lunch I popped into the library. Mrs. K. was wearing a hot-pink dress and platform shoes, her hair wild and curly in a big mass that bounced as she walked.

"Hi, Mrs. K. I loved the book you lent me!" I said.

"Oh, yes. Mm-hmm. A classic. Yes, indeedy. Good, good. She pioneered the genre of modern food writing."

"I can see that. My mom read her in college."

"Ah, yes. As did I."

She had such a quirky way of talking, but you got used to it after a while.

"I have a question. Do you have any info on summer programs in this area? Like camps or classes?" I asked.

"Oh yes, absolutely. Right over here. Come along." She clomped across the floor to a filing cabinet and pulled open a drawer. "All here. Here you go. Righty-ho."

I smiled. "Thank you."

Inside the neat files I found camp counselor jobs I could apply for, local certification classes for things like CPR and junior lifeguard, classes at museums and the public library, and more. I glanced at my watch and realized I needed to wrap things up and get to class.

I could hear Mrs. K. coming back, *clomp, clomp, clomp.*

"One more thing, right here. Look at this," she said, pulling a brochure out of a rubber-banded stack. "You can take it. Bring it back if you don't need it, alrighty? Mm-hmm. Okay, then." And she clomped away.

"Thanks!" I whisper-called after her. I didn't have time to look at the brochure, but I slid it into my book bag and dashed to class.

At five thirty on the nose, Mrs. Sato pulled up in front of my mom's house. I was sitting on the front porch, ready to go. My mom was at work, and Tanner was at a friend's for a sleepover (where he'd certainly stay up way too late, as usual, and then he'd come home super cranky the next day, just in time for me to babysit him while my mom worked at the store and avoided his guaranteed tantrum).

"Ali-li!" cried Tamiko out the window of their white Escalade. She was wearing a navy blue beret and a striped sailor shirt, like Mrs. K. had worn the other day. Tamiko was apparently working a French theme.

"Hiiiii!" I hopped off the porch, jogged to the SUV, and climbed in.

"Bonjour!" said Tamiko by way of greeting.

"Sweet outfit," I said, taking in her jeans and ballet flats.

"Merci," said Tamiko. "That means 'thank you' in French."

"Hello, Allie!" said Mrs. Sato.

"Hi, Mrs. Sato! Thanks for picking me up. Thanks for taking us too!"

"My pleasure. It worked out perfectly. Now tell me how things are at that fabulous school of yours!"

Mrs. Sato was really interested in Vista Green because it was all new, and she thought the teaching was more innovative than at MLK, my old school, where Tamiko and Sierra still went. Unfortunately, where the Satos lived was zoned for MLK.

I filled her in on the new 3-D printer we'd gotten, and the robotics club (not that Tamiko was even interested in that stuff, but Mrs. Sato liked to hear it all), and soon we were at the crêpe restaurant in the next town.

"Okay, girls. I'm heading to the fabric store to look at fabrics for the living room, so I'll be about an hour. Call me if you need me in the meantime, or I'll see you back here then, okay?"

"Thanks!" we all agreed.

Tamiko led the way into La Crêperie, the never-changing, been-there-forever crêpe place. Inside, it was decorated like an old-fashioned French bakery. There were wire baker's racks with curlicues on top, all painted white and filled with jars of jam and jelly for sale; white marble countertops; a tiled floor; retro bakery scales; and wire bins with round loaves of bread for sale. Tamiko thought it was all chic, which meant "stylish." I just liked the crêpes.

The hostess seated us at a marble-topped table surrounded by wire café chairs, and she handed us enormous menus. The waiter came, and we ordered *citron pressé*, which was kind of like lemonade. He left a little basket of sliced French bread with cold, bright-yellow butter that was salty and delicious.

I looked at my menu. "How many variations can you make on a crêpe?" I asked, and giggled.

"Endless," said Tamiko, fake-serious.

There were sweet crêpes and savory ones, filled ones and simple ones, meals and snacks, singles and stacks.

"Hmm. Maybe we should do a savory one first, then a sweet one," I suggested.

"Or we could do a sweet one and then a sweet one," Sierra said with a grin.

I pointed my finger at her. "Bingo!"

The waiter returned, and we placed our orders. I started with a lemon sugar crêpe, followed by a chocolate hazelnut one. Tamiko had a mushroom and Swiss cheese one to start, followed by cinnamon sugar. Sierra went rogue. She had vegetable soup first and then the same chocolate hazelnut one I was having.

"Okay, so I was thinking, for Sunday ...," I began as the waiter walked away.

Tamiko and Sierra shared a meaningful glance.

"What?" I asked.

"What?" said Sierra, all innocent.

"Why are you guys looking at each other like that?"

"Like what?" asked Sierra, starting to blush.

I stared at them. "What's going on?"

They were silent, and then Tamiko sighed. "Listen, Allie, we're excited about *Yay Gourmet*. We think your mom deserves tons of credit and praise for what

91

she's created at Molly's. It's awesome. But . . ." Tamiko looked at Sierra for help.

"But what?" I asked, my nerves all sharp and sensitive. "What?"

"We think you're overreacting a little," said Sierra reluctantly.

I stared at them.

"Sorry, but it's true," said Tamiko with a nod.

"What do you mean?" I asked, flushing.

"All the instructions, the controlling-ness . . ."

"The bossy texts . . . ," added Sierra.

My face was flaming red now. "I thought you guys were excited too! Jeez. Fine. What*ever*. You don't even have to come!" I wondered if I should go to the bathroom and text my mom to come pick me up.

"Allie. Stop," said Sierra. "We *are* excited. We're *thrilled*! It's just—"

"You're making us nervous. You're overthinking it," said Tamiko.

"But someone has to!" I said, practically in a wail.

The waiter arrived with our first courses just then. "Voilà!" he said, placing the crêpes and soup on the table with a flourish.

92

"*Merci*," said Tamiko to the waiter, who was as American as we were.

If I hadn't been in a fight with them just then, I would have laughed. It was like a joke, all this pretending we were eating dinner in France.

Sierra placed her hand over mine on the cool marble tabletop. "Allie. I know you think you need to take charge and that your mom's not taking it seriously enough. But she's focused on the important part—the ice cream! That's what they're coming to write about. Not our . . . nails, or whatever."

What they were saying was setting my teeth on edge. No one moved.

"We will do anything to see Molly's succeed," Tamiko said. "We love it almost as much as you do. We've been there from the beginning, since it was just a little *baby* ice cream store. . . ."

"In little ice-cream-store diapers," added Sierra with a smile.

"Drinking from ice-cream-store baby bottles," said Tamiko, laughing.

"Shaking its little baby ice-cream-store rattle," said Sierra, who was also laughing now.

I couldn't help it. I had to laugh too. They kept

on going, stupid stuff about ice-cream-store naps and ice-cream-store blankies and whatever, and pretty soon we were all laughing hysterically while our food grew cold.

"Okay. Stop. Stop. I get it. I'm sorry," I said.

Tamiko dug into her crêpe, and Sierra picked up her soup spoon.

"It's just that I'm so worried that the article could fail. And then what?" I whispered.

"It's not going to fail," said Tamiko.

Sierra shook her head and swallowed her soup. "No way. And you know what? It's not your fault if it does. It's not your responsibility. It's your mom's."

I sighed. "I know. I guess. I just want her to succeed. It's important for my family."

"We know, *chica*," said Sierra. "We'll help."

"It's gonna be awesome!" said Tamiko. "I've got a really great soundtrack ready."

"Which reminds me!" said Sierra. "Tessa wrote this amazing song last week, and we're practicing it tomorrow. I want to send you guys a demo of it. It's so cool."

I sighed. Tessa was the last person I wanted to talk about right then.

I sliced my crêpe harder than necessary, and a piece shot across the table toward Sierra. "Sorry," I said, reaching over to pick it up.

"Tessa is so talented," continued Sierra. "She's also so smart. She skipped second grade, you know."

"Wow!" Tamiko said. I didn't bother to say anything.

Sierra ate a bite of her soup and swallowed, then started singing:

> *"Something electric in the air,*
> *Breeze flowing through my hair,*
> *Hoping you will appear . . ."*

Another love song from Tessa. What a surprise. I imagined her sitting with a guitar, strumming away as she daydreamed about Colin. Suddenly I couldn't bear to listen to the song anymore. "Blah, blah, blah," I muttered.

"What?" asked Sierra, surprised.

"If Tessa's going to make you sing her songs, they should at least be half-*decent*." The words spilled out of my mouth before I could stop myself.

Tamiko and Sierra stared at me.

"Wow, Allie, that was mean," said Tamiko.

I knew Tamiko was right, but the blood had rushed to my head, and I felt like I was about to explode. "I'm just saying the truth," I replied, but it came out snappier than I'd meant it to.

There was a pause. "What's the deal?" Sierra asked.

"Are you still mad about the *Yay Gourmet* thing?" asked Tamiko. She'd finished her mushroom and cheese crêpe and had neatly lined her utensils up on her plate.

"No. I'm just so sick of hearing about Tessa! She's smart, she's popular, she's cool, she's talented, she writes songs for your band, she has pretty hair—"

"But those are all positive qualities!" said Tamiko.

Suddenly Sierra did a facepalm. "OMG!" she said, shaking her head. "How could I be so blind?"

"What?" asked Tamiko.

"It's because Tessa likes Colin!"

"So?" asked Tamiko.

"Allie does too!" said Sierra.

The waiter came to clear the plates away, and we had to just sit there and not talk for a second.

Then Tamiko said, "You *do*?"

I looked down at the table. "I'm not sure," I mumbled.

"Okay, let's start from the beginning," said Sierra.

"I'm gonna need another lemonade!" said Tamiko. *"Serveur!"* She called out the word for "waiter" in French, although I wasn't sure if her pronunciation was correct. The guy didn't even turn around. Then she called, "Waiter!" and he turned around and came right to our table.

We had to laugh.

CHAPTER EIGHT

PILLOW FIGHT!

"So let me get this straight," said Tamiko. "You *might* like Colin. You're not sure. You just don't want Tessa to like him, or him to like Tessa?"

"I guess?" I said. "It sounds so bad when you put it like that."

"Can he like someone else? Not Tessa? Not you? Another girl?"

The words "someone else" rang in my ears from Daniel's comment at Molly's the other day.

"Why? Did you hear that someone else likes him? Or that he likes someone else?" I asked urgently, leaning across the table toward Tamiko.

"No," said Tamiko, widening her eyes at me. "Down, girl."

"It's because she has a crush on him!" insisted Sierra.

"NO!" I said strongly. "Not really. I mean . . . I don't know."

"Tell us how you feel about him," said Tamiko. "Tell Miko, hmm?"

I laughed and rolled my eyes. "It's just . . ." I sighed. "I like sitting on the bus with him in the mornings. Like, I look forward to it."

"Okaaaay," said Tamiko.

"He told his sister about me. Like, she reads my column in the paper."

"Uh-huh," said Sierra encouragingly.

"I get happy when I see him in the newspaper meetings. Well, except for last week, when he didn't like my idea," I said.

"Jerk!" said Tamiko.

"No. It was . . . It was a bad idea, actually. It wasn't smart. I didn't skip second grade like some people."

Sierra swatted me, and I laughed.

"What else?" prompted Tamiko.

"He told me he liked my new headband the other day. Like, he noticed it was new and said he liked it. And after I didn't see him for a few days, when I saw him again, he said he'd missed me."

Sierra and Tamiko both raised their eyebrows and nodded meaningfully at each other.

"Stop!" I laughed.

"Well, one thing's for sure," said Tamiko. "He likes *you*, sistah!"

"Yeah. Guys do *not* notice headbands on girls they don't crush on," agreed Sierra. She and Tamiko high-fived.

"But I think he likes Tessa. Patrick said—"

Tamiko waved her hand in the air. "Buzz, buzz, buzz. Who cares what Patrick says!"

"Okay, well, Daniel said—"

"Uh-uh, no way," said Sierra.

"Well, then, I saw them together on Sunday!" I blurted.

"Oh," said Tamiko.

"Hmm," said Sierra. "What were they doing?"

"I don't know. Walking. Taking the bus?"

"Did it seem date-y?" Tamiko asked, narrowing her eyes critically.

I sighed. "I don't know. I mean, I assumed so. What else would they be doing?"

"Look," said Sierra. "You aren't even sure you like him. But you're jealous of Tessa. Here's what my mom says when Isa and I are feeling jealous: 'Stop being jealous, and instead spend your energy on being the best *you* that you can be.'"

"Hmm," I said. "What's that supposed to mean?"

"Like, when I used to get jealous that Isa was better at soccer. And I'd spend all my time obsessively watching her instead of practicing myself! And she'd get better while I'd get worse! But actually, in the end, I had to admit that she was really good, and I . . . wasn't that good but also wasn't that interested in soccer anyway."

"So what do I do?"

Of course, right then the waiter arrived with the bill. We waited until he was gone.

"Focus on your friendship with Colin. You've got that going on," said Sierra.

"And the whole newspaper thing," added Tamiko.

"And don't worry about Tessa," said Sierra.

"Right. What she said," said Tamiko.

I sighed. "I'll try." Anne of Green Gables popped into my mind, unbidden: *It's been my experience that you can nearly always enjoy things if you make up your mind firmly that you will!*

Oh, Anne! I thought. *Why do you always have to be right?*

We all decided to sleep at Tamiko's that night. Mrs. Sato very nicely let me and Sierra stop by our houses to grab a few things. I took my books out of my backpack, grabbed the polka-dot headband Colin liked to show it to them and the M.F.K. Fisher book, and jammed my overnight stuff into my backpack.

At Tamiko's she showed us all the sneakers she was customizing in her craft room, or "studio," as she called it. They were amazing. There was one pair she was painting in camouflage with "flocked" paint, so the paint looked furry. There was another pair she was embroidering with flowers using a heavy-duty needle and embroidery thread. A third pair was getting bedazzled with rivets and "gem" studs, and there was one last pair that she was trying to scent by spraying them with cinnamon spray every day for a week. (They reeked.)

"These are awesome, Miko," I said. "I'm impressed. You've been very busy being the best you that you can be."

Later we watched a movie and had popcorn with Parmesan cheese on it; then we headed up to bed.

As Tamiko was blowing up an air mattress for me, I unpacked my bathroom kit, and something flew out of my bag. I stooped to pick it up and saw the flyer Mrs. K. had given me earlier. I stopped for a minute and looked at it.

"Teen Classes," it said.

Ho hum, I thought. *Bor-ing!*

But Sierra was in the bathroom getting ready, so I sat on Tamiko's bed for a minute and flipped through the brochure. It was actually pretty cool.

There were the usual sporty offerings: dance, gymnastics, swimming, soccer, basketball, all at the town YMCA. Then there was stuff like language classes, writing courses—summer-school kinds of stuff.

No thanks, I thought.

But toward the back were "Pre-Professional Classes," and that was where things started to get interesting.

"Hey, Tamiko," I said. "Did you know there are fashion design classes being offered in town this summer?"

"What?" asked Tamiko. "Where?"

"At the high school, at night. They bring in real

fashion people and show you how to do stuff like make patterns, design fabric, all kinds of things. It looks really cool."

Tamiko came over to where I was sitting and peered over my shoulder. "Wow. That looks interesting. Ooh, and look at the photography classes. I could get into that big-time."

I turned a page. "And there's cooking stuff too. Like cake decorating, candy making, and, hey! Ice cream making. My mom could teach that!"

Sierra came in from the bathroom in the hall. "What is it?"

I showed her the flyer.

"Summer school?" she asked.

"Kind of, but cooler," I said. I was still scanning the pages. "Hey! They have food writing." I looked up at them. "Food writing is pretty great, actually. The librarian, Mrs. K.—remember I told you about her?—she gave me this book." I leaned over and pulled it out of my backpack. "It's pretty interesting. It's, like, professional food writing."

"Kind of like *Yay Gourmet*?" asked Sierra, her eyes twinkling.

"Exactly!"

"Well, maybe you should take that class. It might help you with your ice cream newspaper column. You do seem obsessed with food writing, after all!" teased Tamiko.

I picked my pillow up from the air mattress and whacked her with it. She grabbed her pillow and whacked me back. Soon we were all three in a major pillow fight that ended only when Mr. Sato came to tell us to settle down.

Just for the record: *I won.*

We stayed up way too late and then slept until nine, so the next day I was running behind and was tired. Once I was home, I made myself an egg sandwich with sriracha and dove into my homework. At around ten my mom came home and dropped Tanner off, then headed to work. He was grumpy and took to the couch to watch cartoons while I did my homework in my room.

At noon I went out to see what he wanted for lunch. I was thinking grilled cheese and chocolate milk. But he was sound asleep on the sofa. His cheeks were bright red, and he was bent at an uncomfortable angle, but still he was out cold. I tried to wake him up to at least take off his jeans and get him into bed, but I couldn't wake him up.

By one o'clock I was nervous. Tanner was still asleep and flushed. I called my mom at the store.

"Oh, sweetheart! I'm so busy, and Rashid's swamped at the counter. What's up?"

I told her about Tanner, and she gasped. "Can you take his temperature and call me right back?"

I hung up and did what she'd asked. Tanner was super groggy, but I got the thermometer into his mouth and waited until it beeped.

The thermometer said 103.5 degrees.

"Oh no," I whispered. I ran back to the phone and called my mom at the store. My heart was beating hard and fast in my chest, and my hands were cold with fear. "Mom! He has a fever of a hundred and three and a half!"

"Oh no! Oh, the poor boy!" my mom cried. Then I heard her take a deep breath. "Listen, Allie, I've got my hands full and I can't leave the store. Your dad's away on a business trip, and I don't know when he's coming back. I'm going to call the doctor right now, but you need to give Tanner some medicine, okay?"

I felt my stomach sinking. I had to take care of Tanner myself? "Okay, Mom," I said meekly.

"Thank you so much, Allie. I'm so sorry to put you in this position. I'll try to get home as soon as possible. Also, try to get him to drink as much water as possible, okay? Lots and lots of water."

"Right. Got it," I said.

I managed to get the medicine into Tanner. He took a few sips of water, then fell asleep again. I sat next to him on the sofa and kept waking him up so that he could take more sips. Soon he began to shiver and sweat. Then he became alert. After an hour had passed, he was wide awake and perky, and I took his temperature again. It read one hundred degrees.

"Phew!" I said, looking at the numbers in relief.

My mom had called three times while I'd been sitting with Tanner. The first time she had told me what the doctor had said—Tanner should take medicine, drink lots of fluids, and rest, and then we should see how he felt. Each time I'd filled her in on Tanner's symptoms. Now I called her with the news that his fever had dropped.

"Thank goodness. I was just about to close the

store and come home. I'm so grateful to you for taking care of him. Thank you, sweetheart!"

"It's no problem, Mom," I said, even though I felt exhausted. "I'm just glad he's better."

"Right," she said cautiously. "I hope he's better."

"What do you mean?" I asked. "His temperature went way down."

"Yes, but that's the medicine. The decrease might just be temporary. His temp could go right back up when the medicine wears off."

"Well, *then* what?"

"We just keep an eye on him, give him more medicine, have him rest . . ."

"Until when?"

"Um, until he's better. Or we can take him to the walk-in clinic."

"Like, tomorrow?" I asked, almost not daring to entertain the idea.

"Yes."

"What about . . . *Yay Gourmet*?" I whispered.

My mom sighed. "One of us will have to stay home with him."

"Me," I said flatly.

"Let's just cross that bridge *if* we come to it, okay?"

"Right," I said. "Okay, bye." Then I put down the phone.

I texted my friends the news, and they were appropriately horrified, offering to stay with Tanner themselves so that I could be at the store for *Yay Gourmet*.

Thanks, I replied. Let's cross that bridge if we come to it, I said, quoting my mom.

CHAPTER NINE

HEATING UP

I watched the whole fever cycle unfold. Tanner was peppy, then Tanner was quiet, then Tanner's cheeks were red again, then Tanner fell asleep. Tanner's temperature was back up to 103.

My mom had Rashid call Daphne to come help at the store, and then she canceled her plans for her girls' night out and came home. She rushed into Tanner's room and knelt down by the sofa, feeling his forehead and kissing him. She looked at me with worried eyes.

"He's sick. I think I'd better cancel tomorrow," she said.

"Mom! No! You can't!"

She sighed and leaned back on her heels. "But if

he's not better tomorrow, I've got to take him to the doctor, and then one of us needs to stay home with him."

"I can," I said, even though it nearly killed me to spit out the bitter words.

She shook her head. "You're as much a part of Molly's as I am. You need to be there."

"Why don't you just ask Dad to come home from his trip?" I said.

She pursed her lips in a line and looked to the side, thinking. "I really don't want to do that," she said.

"Mom! It's an emergency!"

She took a deep breath. "Fine. You know what? I will. It can't hurt to ask, right?"

"Right!" I encouraged her. I followed my mom out to the hall and sat on the stairs just below her while she called my dad. I leaned my head against her knees as she spoke quietly to him, and I sat there feeling grateful that my parents got along better than ever now that they were divorced. They really seemed like friends. Kinda funny.

After a bit she hung up and sighed again.

"So?" I asked.

"He's going to try to get on the next flight home."

"Awesome!"

"He's not sure he'll be able to, though."

"Oh."

We sat quietly on the stairs for a few minutes, my mom playing with my hair. It was relaxing. Then she stood up. "I'm going to warm up some soup for us all, okay?"

"Okay."

We walked downstairs to the kitchen.

"Allie?"

"Yes?"

"You're a great kid. What would I do without you?" She gave me an enormous hug. Then she pulled away and held my shoulders with her hands as she looked at me. "I'm sorry that I give you so much responsibility. I know it seems like I'm not totally in control sometimes, like with the *Yay Gourmet* thing, or at home, but . . . this co-parenting is a work in progress. And I think I get the important stuff right, right?"

I nodded.

"Thanks to you and Tanner," she said, hugging me again. "Look. It's not that we can prevent things from going wrong in life. That's just not possible. What matters is how we handle them when they do. Right?"

"Right."

We turned in early, my mom sleeping in Tanner's extra bed so that she could keep an eye on him. Before I got into my pj's, I laid out my outfit for tomorrow just in case. I felt exhausted, but I couldn't fall asleep right away. I knew it wasn't Tanner's fault that he had a fever. It wasn't my dad's fault that he had a business trip, either. But I had worked so hard preparing for the *Yay Gourmet* interview, and just thinking about missing it made tears spring to my eyes.

I woke up the next morning when my alarm went off at seven thirty. I hit snooze, and it went off again, what felt like only seconds later. I had slept so soundly through the night that I was disoriented when I woke up. I thought I was still dreaming because I could hear my parents talking in the kitchen downstairs.

Suddenly I sat bolt upright in my bed.

"Dad?" I called.

The voices downstairs stopped.

I realized Tanner might still be sleeping, so I flung off my covers and quickly tiptoed out of my room and down the stairs. As I turned the corner, I saw my dad in a suit sitting at the counter drinking coffee.

"Daddy!" I squealed. I couldn't help it. I burst into tears and ran into his arms. He hugged me tightly and patted my back and didn't let go.

"I was so scared," I wailed into his shoulder.

"Shh. It's okay. Mom and I are here. Everything's fine." He kept patting my back and hushing me. "It's all right."

"I was so worried," I told him. "I didn't think you were going to get here in time."

My dad smiled down at me. "I know how important this is to your mom . . . and to you," he said. "And when something is important to you, I will always do everything in my power to help."

I gave him an extra hard squeeze.

Then there was another voice in the doorway.

"Dad?"

It was Tanner, all bright-eyed and bushy-tailed, as my mom would have said.

"Hey, buddy!" said my dad, holding out an arm so that Tanner could join us.

Tanner scrambled onto my dad's lap and nestled in.

My mom was watching us wistfully from the other side of the kitchen island.

"Come on, Mom," said my dad.

And my mom didn't even hesitate. She came right around the island, and we had a big family hug, just like we used to. It felt amazing.

"We're still a family," said my dad.

I was so happy, but it made me want to cry harder, and I could *not* have puffy eyes for the photo shoot!

I pulled away and went to wash my face in the kitchen sink. "Mom! We have to get going! The cleaners and the window washers!" I said.

"I already let them in," she said.

"You did? What time?"

"Six?" she said, squinting at the clock.

"Wow. Good job, Mom."

"Allie! I'm pretty competent! As much as I appreciate your help, I *can* survive without you bossing me." She laughed.

"Yes, but everything would not go as smoothly," I said.

She laughed again. "Maybe not. But maybe they'd just go differently."

"Okay, gang. Time to get this show on the road, I think," said my dad.

"Showers," said my mom.

"I go first!" said Tanner.

"Mom!" I complained.

"Hey," Dad said to Tanner. "You and I are going to Molly's later. Let's let the ladies get ready first, since they have to be there early to work. You and I are just going as customers, so we don't have to look fancy. Okay?"

"What do you mean?" Tanner asked.

"I mean we're just there to eat ice cream, so we don't have to be early or get dressed up! We can hang out here!" Dad replied.

"And play video games?" asked Tanner hopefully.

"You betcha!" said my dad.

"Yessss!" said Tanner, pumping his fist. "This is the best day ever!"

My mom and I rolled our eyes at each other. We hated video games, and Tanner was always begging us to play with him.

"Just one more temperature, baby," said my mom to Tanner. When the thermometer beeped, we all leaned in to read it.

"One hundred. Much better!" said my mom.

"On the mend!" said my dad.

"Let's go!" I said, and dashed up the stairs. We were meeting Tamiko and Sierra at the Salon on the Square for our hair and makeup (we'd realized that would be easier than having my mom's friend Annie lug all her gear over to Molly's), and we didn't have time to spare.

When Annie was finished, our blowouts looked amazing, and in our dresses we all looked like we were going to a party. The makeup consisted of clear mascara and clear lip gloss that Annie let us take with us so that we could "freshen up between takes," whatever that meant.

Now, as calm as my mom had been leading up to this day, it was as if she had reserved all her panic for the last minute. She ran around the store like a crazy person once we got there, arranging flowers she'd bought, wiping up tables that were already clean, fussing with the toilet paper in the bathroom.

"Mom, I don't think *Yay Gourmet* is coming to photograph the bathroom!" I called after her.

She popped her head back out and laughed. "I

know, but you can tell so much about a place by how clean its bathroom is!"

Soon we opened for business, and right then the reporter and photographer arrived.

The reporter, Maryann, was a petite woman with tiny dreadlocks. The photographer, Anita, was a taller lady with lots of scarves on, including one wrapped in a turban around her head. They were both super-nice, but we were all really, really nervous.

My mom showed Maryann around the store while Anita started testing all the lights, flipping them on and off.

"I feel like we're at a disco party," said Tamiko quietly.

We giggled nervously.

Anita said, "I'm just going to get some lighting equipment from my van up the street. I'll be right back."

"I'll help you!" offered Tamiko, and she came out from behind the counter.

"Thank you so much! Why, aren't you the cutest thing?"

"Yes, I am the cutest thing," joked Tamiko, all fake-modestly.

Anita threw her head back and let out a giant laugh, and then those two were best friends for the rest of the day.

Tamiko was really interested in photography, so she was actually very into helping Anita. When they came back a little later with a bunch of reflectors and a floor light, they were chatting away. Anita was explaining lighting basics to Tamiko, and Tamiko was asking tons of questions.

"Looks like she's in her happy place," said Sierra, gesturing at Tamiko.

"Totally," I agreed.

Maryann and my mom had finished the tour and were chatting quietly at one of the tables. By now it was eleven o'clock and customers were starting to trickle in. I wished more people would come so that Anita and Maryann could see how popular we were!

The girls and I scooped and rang, and Anita shot candid photos of us while we worked. We all tried to look as good as possible, scooping with smiles on our faces, the headbands I handed out perfectly in place, and making each ice cream order a work of art. Anita snapped away.

The bell started to jingle more frequently as the

early-lunch crowd of mostly little kids and their parents began to arrive. Tanner and my dad came by, and Anita got some shots of Tanner eating a cone as big as his head, and some with my parents and me too. Now the door was jingling and the register was ringing sales, and Maryann had joined us behind the counter to "get a feel for it all."

I called out to Sierra to ring up an order. Sierra, Cookies and C—"

"Colin!" she whispered.

"No, Cream!" I said, confused. "Cookies and Cream."

"No! Colin's here!"

What? I turned and saw him walking through the door with some friends. Guy friends. I searched for any sign of Tessa, but I didn't see her. Phew!

He saw me and smiled and came right up to the counter. "Hey!" he said.

"Hey!" I said. "Thanks for coming!"

"Wouldn't have missed it for the world! I know how important this is for you—and for Molly's! And I am your number one customer, after all. Is that *them*?" he asked quietly, jutting his chin slightly toward Maryann and Anita, who were speaking with my mom.

I looked and then turned back to him. "Yup."

"Nice?" he asked.

"Very," I said.

"Good. Can I order something, please?"

"What'll it be? No flower flavors, I know," I whispered with a smile.

"Shh!" he joked. "Hmmm." Colin scanned the menu. "I'll have . . . the Banana Pudding shake, please."

"Wait! What about Cereal Milk? I thought *that* was your favorite?"

"Really? Did I say that? That must've been my favorite *last* week. Now I'm into Banana Pudding."

"Huh," I said. "Me too."

I made his shake, set it to mix, and then went back to chat with him at the counter.

"Listen, I owe you an apology," he said. "I forgot to say it when I saw you the other day."

"What for?" I asked.

"I wasn't very supportive of your idea at the last newspaper meeting. I didn't treat you nicely, like a real friend, and I felt terrible afterward. I . . . Oh gosh." He put his hand over his eyes. "I actually *didn't* forget to apologize the other day, as a matter of fact. I just . . . We hadn't seen each other for a bit, and then we were having such a nice time again that I didn't want to bring it up in case you'd get mad."

I was quiet for a second as I decided what to say. Part of me wanted to just laugh it off and act like it hadn't been a big deal. But that would have dishonored our friendship and his kind apology. He *had* read the situation right. I *had* been hurt by what he'd said in the meeting. Now he was making up for it.

"I accept your apology," I said.

Colin smiled. "Thanks. Sometimes I feel like I have to sort of show off for the editor in chief in meetings, now that I'm the assistant editor. Like, I have to act like I know what I'm doing. And sometimes I don't do it right."

"It's okay. Anyway, I owe you an apology too."

"Why?"

I took a deep breath. "I was really weird when I ran into you and Tessa last week."

"Yeah! You *were* really weird. What was up with that?"

I sighed. "I just . . . felt left out. Like you and I are supposed to be friends, and then there you were with some friend I don't even know, and she seems to know you better than I do, even, and . . . I felt awkward or . . . jealous or something." I looked away.

"Oh," said Colin. "Well, you were weird, but I wasn't upset. I don't even know Tessa that well. We just take tennis at the same place, and our moms organized for us to take the bus home together since we live in the same neighborhood. I think my friend Patrick actually has a crush on her."

"Really?" My knees felt weak with relief. I felt so silly. Why had I worried and assumed that Colin and Tessa were a couple?

"Yeah, so—" Colin was saying.

Suddenly there was a crash. I turned to see a unicorn sundae splattered all over the floor, all over a customer, all over the front of the ice cream freezer.

"Oh no!" I breathed in horror.

CHAPTER TEN

UNICORN DOWN!

Sierra was aghast, her hands still open in midair where the sundae had fallen from them.

I rushed to the sink, and as I did, I said calmly, "Tamiko. Mop, please. Sierra, take a deep breath and start making a new sundae." I grabbed a roll of paper towels and started soaking bunches of them in warm water. Then I quickly handed them to the customer.

Luckily the sundae had only caught the customer on the legs, and she was wearing shorts and flip-flops. The lady laughed it off and mopped off her feet and shins.

Sierra, on the other hand, was traumatized. She looked like she was going to cry.

"I'm sorry, Allie! I'm so sorry! I'm so sorry!" she

whispered in horror. "And the *Yay Gourmet* people are here!"

Some people remain calm and then grow panicky in a crisis. I panic leading up to big events but grow calm if anything goes wrong. "Sierra, do *not* worry. It was an accident. Make the new sundae and make it really good," I said quietly. "Go on."

Sierra followed my orders and moved like a robot. I stole a glance at Anita, Maryann, and my mom, and they were all watching quietly as Tamiko and Sierra and I handled the debacle.

Colin and his friends had retreated to the far table and, I noticed, were calmly chatting and eating and acting as if nothing unusual had happened. I was so grateful to Colin for managing that. Other boys might have laughed and pointed and made a scene, but these guys didn't, and I knew it was Colin's leadership that had kept them in line.

Soon everything was under control. The store was clean, the customer was clean, and she was devouring her new sundae with pleasure.

Things had quieted down, and Anita asked if now would be a good time for her to get some "product shot" photos of the ice cream itself. We said yes and started to assemble our planned sample menu.

I went into the back and got the tray of perfect Lime Sorbet scoops out of the Deepfreeze. I rolled them off the parchment paper and into a bowl that I'd left near the freezer. As I turned to bring the scoops to the front, I spied Tamiko's phone plugged into the sound system for the store. Quickly I put down the bowl and scrolled through her music until I found a Wildflowers playlist. I selected it and pushed play. Then I quickly brought the lime scoops out front.

Tamiko and Sierra noticed the music and stopped, their mouths open in surprise. Then they turned to me, smiling.

"Thanks, Allie," said Sierra. "Thanks so much."

Tamiko winked at me.

I looked at my friends and beamed in gratitude for them. Then I began to assemble the lime cones and stand them in the cone rack on top of the counter.

Anita snapped a couple shots of the Lime Sorbet cones as I put them up, but she didn't seem very into it. She took one or two snaps of the Rockin' Rocky Road cones that Sierra made, but again, she wasn't going crazy like paparazzi at the Oscars.

My friends and I exchanged perplexed looks. What was up?

Finally Tamiko arrived with the most perfect, gorgeous-looking unicorn sundae I'd ever seen. Sierra and I even oohed and aahed over it. She presented it to Anita and stepped back, her hands clasped proudly in front of her chest.

Anita smiled politely and took one or two shots, then put down her camera. She took a deep breath. "Girls. These are beautiful confections, worthy of an Austrian patisserie. They are flawless!"

We all relaxed and smiled. She got it.

"But . . ."

But? There was a "but"?

". . . they look too good to eat."

We looked at one another in confusion. That didn't even make sense.

Maryann stood up and came over. "What Anita means is, well, we can see how hard you've worked and how perfect everything is. But ice cream . . . It's a messy food. It's for kids, really, and it's an indulgence. It isn't something that you eat primly. And your mom's flavors . . . Molly's flavors . . . They're anything but prim and proper! They're wild and passionate and messy and inventive!"

"They make us hungry!" said Anita with a laugh.

My mom joined us. "Thanks!" she said.

"Can you . . . Could I ask you to do some messy cones?" asked Anita. "Something really yummy and appetizing, with dribbles? A sundae with fudge and marshmallows spilling over the sides, the ice cream half melted? Maybe a bite taken out of it?"

Maryann added, "We need texture. We want our readers to imagine what the ice cream would taste like. And to convey that, we've got to make the photos as authentic as possible. Like our readers are right here. Does that make sense?"

My friends and I smiled at one another. "I think it *does*!" I said.

Quickly we set about making gooey, messy cones, with multiple scoops of our favorite flavors, scoops that dripped and melted down our wrists. Anita had us all loosen our hair and line up behind the counter and take huge bites of cones right at the same time. It was a feast. We were all laughing and having fun.

And the new unicorn sundae was a triumph!

Tamiko put in her favorite flavors—Saint Louis Cake and Banana Pudding—then smothered the scoops with hot fudge and caramel that oozed down the sides of the ice cream. The dish was overflowing and making a sticky puddle on the marble tabletop where it sat. Anita moved around the table like she was photographing a movie star. She had Tamiko hold the light reflector for her while she made commentary like a celebrity photographer on TV. "Wonderful! Delicious! Fabulous!" she said as she shot.

After they were done, Maryann copied all our names down and showed them to us to make sure she had the spellings correct. Then she gave an embarrassed smile. "I've had a lot of amazing tastes of ice cream today, but—well, I'm ready for a scoop of my own now, please."

"Absolutely!" said Sierra, rushing to get behind the counter. "What can I make for you?"

Maryann combined Lime Sorbet with Balsamic Strawberry, and Sierra went to scoop it, saying, "*Yay Gourmet!*" which made everyone laugh. Anita got into it too and asked for Banana Pudding with hot fudge in a dish, which Tamiko prepared.

"Don't forget the sprinkle of happy!" said Tamiko. They each put a pinch of rainbow sprinkles on top and gave the ice cream to the ladies.

My mom said we helpers should all have our own as well, and soon the six of us were sitting in a cluster of chairs around a table, and we were telling Anita and Maryann our summer plans, with Tamiko mentioning the photo classes and the food writing classes we were thinking of taking. I mentioned M.F.K. Fisher, and Maryann was so excited, saying that Fisher had been a huge inspiration for her and had played a role in her becoming a food writer. Both Anita and Maryann remarked on the music, and we told them all about the Wildflowers and Sierra's talent. They were super-impressed.

After a bit the post-lunch crowd began to dribble in, and it meant the tidal wave was coming soon. We cleaned up and began to say our good-byes to Anita and Maryann.

Maryann shook our hands warmly and said, "I can't begin to tell you how impressed I am by you young ladies. You are such a good team, and you flow so well—even in a crisis."

"Thanks," I said. "Someone wise once told me

not to worry about things we couldn't control. We can't prevent things from going wrong, but we can control how we react when they do."

"That *is* a very wise person," said Maryann with a smile.

Anita hugged us all, and she and Tamiko exchanged contact information. It seemed like Tamiko was really interested in food photography after today. Maybe she'd just enjoyed making a mess in the shop for a change.

My mom took the ladies outside to say good-bye and so Anita could get some shots of her in front of the store, and my friends and I took a minute to do a silent scream of happiness.

"It went so well, you guys!" I said in a quiet, happy voice. "Thank you so much! I'm so psyched!"

"It was all thanks to your organizing," said Sierra kindly.

"You mean my control-freaking?"

"You're not a control freak," said Tamiko. "You're detail-oriented."

I laughed. "That makes it sound better. Seriously, though, we couldn't have done it without you guys. I wouldn't have wanted to do it without you guys."

"Thanks for having us. It was fun!" said Tamiko.

"Yeah, I really enjoyed it," Sierra added.

My mom came in a little bit later, and we were on a roll with the afternoon rush. She gave us each a hug and tucked some extra cash into our pockets as a thank-you, and for the time we'd put in at the beginning of the day.

"We had a great time, Mrs. S.," said Tamiko between customers.

"I would have been bummed if we'd missed it," agreed Sierra.

"You girls were so impressive!" crowed my mom. "I can't thank you all enough. I'm going to go sit down in the back with a cup of coffee for a minute. Then I'll let you all go home a little early."

"We want to stay," said Tamiko.

"Yeah," agreed Sierra.

I shrugged. "Me too."

My mom laughed. "Okay! I'll see you in a little bit, then."

As the late-afternoon rush died down into the pre-dinner lull, my friends and I did our usual Sunday evening routine. We refilled the toppings from buckets in the fridge, in the freezer, and on the shelves. We wiped down all the tables and counters. Tamiko restocked the cups, straws, cones, and dishes. I cleaned the (yuck) bathroom.

After Sierra's parents came to pick up Tamiko and Sierra and drive them home, my mom came out to chat with me. It was quiet in the store, and I was going to leave soon.

"Allie, I hadn't heard that idea about the food writing camp this summer. I think it sounds wonderful!"

"Oh, yeah, well, I took your advice. I went to Mrs. K., and she gave me a ton of info about lots of programs and jobs and internships I could do in town. I think the food writing sounds cool, if you're okay with it."

"I'll talk to your dad, but I think it would be perfect for you. And fun if Tamiko's taking photography there as well!"

I nodded. My summer was coming together. One less thing for me to worry about.

"Okay, run on home now. Relieve Dad from Tanner's video games, please, okay?"

"Uh-huh." I went over and gave my mom a giant hug. "It was a great day, mom."

"I'm so proud of you," she whispered into my hair.

"I'm so proud of you, Mom. You've created something really cool here. I'm happy that the world is noticing."

She squeezed me tighter. "Thank you, sweetheart."

CHAPTER ELEVEN

EXTRA, EXTRA!

It was a week later when my mom texted me at school, two words: It's out.

I knew what she meant and quickly typed back, Can't wait!

The *Yay Gourmet* article about Molly's had been posted, and my mom and I had agreed to read it together. I raced to the store after school and barreled in the door.

"I'm here, I'm here. You didn't cheat, did you?"

My mother shook her head. "Nope. I promised I'd wait."

I squealed and rubbed my hands together. "Let's do it!"

We sat at a table, and my mom opened the *Yay*

Gourmet home page in her browser, and there it was, at the top of the site:

Molly's Ice Cream

Gooey and Old-Fashioned, Just Like Grandma Used to Make

Tart Balsamic Strawberry, rich and creamy Banana Pudding, sour Lime Sorbet, chunky and chocolaty Rockin' Rocky Road . . . These are just a few of the excellent and innovative flavors that the ice cream alchemist Meg Shear has crafted at Molly's, her fresh and stylish ice cream parlor where everything old is new again. Or is everything new old again? No matter! The ice cream is captivating.

With top-of-the-line ingredients; a traditional hand-churning process that creates dense, almost chewy cream bases; and flavors that only a mad scientist or a very brilliant five-year-old could create

(Gingerbread House or Cereal Milk, anyone?), Molly's delivers a consistently scrumptious product.

"OMG, Mom! This is amazing!" I cried, looking up from the screen.

The article continued on to rave about the store's decor ("an immaculate retro vibe reminiscent of Walt Disney World's Confectionery on Main Street, USA") and the "vibrant young ice-creamistas who scoop and serve, offering a 'sprinkle of happy' on top of each order."

"That's us, Mom!" I said, feeling goose bumps of excitement. I read on, scrolling through the photos of oozing cones and dribbly sundaes. There was a pretty photo of my mom outside the store, shot from a cool low angle; a cute little snap of Tanner (wiping his mouth on his sleeve!); and then, at the very end, a wide and big shot of me and my besties, eating our messy cones behind the counter in our headbands, and laughing.

"Oh, Allie, what a beautiful photo that is of you three. I'll have to see if I can get Anita to send me a copy to frame for everyone's parents."

"Mom! Look at the caption! It has our names!"

"'A sprinkle of happy,'" she read aloud. "'Tamiko

Sato, Allie Shear, and Sierra Perez enjoy a rare break from serving the masses.'"

"Mom. Do you realize? Maryann got it all right!"

My mom smiled. "You're right!"

"Even our names!"

"She was a very nice lady."

I sighed happily. "Let's read it again!" I said.

We scrolled to the beginning and read it three more times, admiring the photos each time and noticing new details.

"It's great writing, don't you think?" said my mom.

I agreed. "She's not M.F.K. Fisher, but she's close!"

"Hey, that reminds me, we've got to get to the library this weekend and check out some food writing, okay? Saturday?"

I nodded. "Great."

Then my mom wanted to write a thank-you e-mail to Maryann right away. It was quiet, so I sent the article to my BFFs.

The door jingled, and a nice-looking man came in wearing a suit.

"Hello. Welcome to Molly's," I said.

"Hi! I'm looking for Meg Shear. Is she available, please?"

"Can I tell her who's asking?"

"Sure. I'm Jim Nichols from the *Daily Chronicle* We'd like to do a story for our food section." He handed me his business card.

My jaw wanted to drop, but I stayed composed. "Certainly. I'll be right back. Can I get you a scoop while you wait?"

He grinned like a kid. "Well, since you asked, I'd love to try the Cereal Milk. I've heard so much about it."

"Sure! Would you like a cup or a cone? Any toppings?"

I prepared his order and handed it to him.

"On the house," I said.

"No, no. Journalists can't accept free things! We have to pay, or people won't think we're impartial!" he said with a wink.

"Oh, right!" I got it. I rang him up and went to get my mom.

She was staring dreamily at the computer with the ghost of a smile on her face. I quickly whisper-explained who was out front, and she sat up straight and finger-combed her hair behind her ears.

"He's fun too, for a grown-up," I added quietly. "And nice. Really nice."

"Allie, just remember, they won't all be as nice as Maryann and Anita. It's just . . . statistically unlikely. We were lucky for our first big article, but we might not be so lucky again. You can't take it personally. It's just business." She stood and smoothed down her apron.

I nodded.

"How do I look?" she asked.

"Like a million bucks!" I said.

She laughed and gave me a squeeze.

While my mom and Jim Nichols chatted, I grabbed my phone and copied the *Yay. Gourmet* story link. I pasted it into a text message and then hesitated before typing in a contact. It was to Colin. My thumb hovered over the send button. Was it bragging if I sent it to him? Was I being pushy, referencing the story idea he had killed at the newspaper meeting? Maybe Molly's hadn't come off as well as I'd thought and he'd think the article was boring!

Oh, whatever. He was my friend. He'd love it! I pressed send, and then spotted the replies from my besties.

AHHH! YAAAY . . . GOURMET! <3 <3 <3, said Sierra.

Sprinkle Sundays sisters forever! #famous, texted Tamiko.

Then there was a reply from Colin: Amazing! You crushed it! We need to celebrate!

I grinned, and my heart leapt a little as I sent back a text with a smiley face emoji and Thanks!

My phone buzzed again. It was the besties, still going.

Seriously, we look like models. Tamiko Sato is now available for professional photo shoots!

Don't get carried away, Tamiko :D, Sierra texted.

It's not my fault I'm so beautiful, OK?

I laughed. As fun as it was trying to decide if I had a crush on Colin or not, everything always came back to me and my best friends. We were always there for one another, and we always would be, through crushes, spilled sundaes, bad rock band lyrics, French food, and more.

Friendship: so old-fashioned that it's new again. #SprinkleSundaysSisters

DON'T MISS BOOK 8:

BANANA SPLITS

"I need another Bird's Nest Sundae with strawberry ice cream, please!" I called to Allie.

"Bird's Nest Sundae, coming right up!" Allie replied.

I watched my friend make the sundae: one scoop of chocolate ice cream, topped with shredded coconut, jelly beans, and one of those marshmallow birds. The result looked like a bird sitting on its eggs in a nest, and I absolutely loved it. It was my latest sundae creation, and it was probably one of my favorites yet.

The customers loved it too. I'd been counting sales of the new sundae ever since I'd started taking orders at twelve forty-five, and in just two hours we'd sold thirteen of them!

Allie handed me the sundae, which I finished off with a Molly's Ice Cream trademark: a shower of sprinkles.

"Here's your sprinkle of happy," I said, with my best salesgirl smile, handing the sundae to the woman who had ordered it. The little girl next to her began to jump up and down in excitement.

"Ice cream! Ice cream!" she shouted.

"Calm down, Sophie," her mom said patiently. "I just need to pay, and then we'll sit down."

I laughed. "It's okay. We all feel that way about ice cream," I told her, and the woman gave me a grateful smile and made her way to pay my friend Sierra at the register.

I spun around to Allie. "Thirteen in two hours!" I bragged.

"I was counting too. That might be a record," she said. Then she scrunched up her freckly nose in that way she does when she's thinking. "I wonder if it *is* a record. Why haven't we ever thought about keeping stats on this kind of thing?"

"We could, if we input flavors into the computer

system," Sierra chimed in, tapping the register. "Right now it only keeps track of small sundae, medium sundae, small cone, like that."

"This sounds like a job for Sierra Perez, math genius," I said, wiggling my eyebrows.

"That might be beyond my genius capabilities," Sierra answered. "But I'll talk to your mom about it, Allie."

"Awesome!" Allie replied.

Allie's mom, Mrs. S., owns Molly's Ice Cream, which is named after her grandmother. Allie, Sierra, and I have been besties since we were tiny, and we work together in the shop every Sunday afternoon. I'm glad we do, because Allie's parents got divorced last summer and now Allie goes to a different school from Sierra and me. Most weeks, our Sprinkle Sundays are the only day we're all together in the same place.

I gazed around at the shop. Three teenage girls were sitting on stools at the high counter that faces the window. A dad and his two little boys were eating ice cream cones at one of the small round tables, and at the table next to them, Sophie was digging into her Bird's Nest Sundae while her mom watched.

I wiped my hands on my apron. "I'm going to take a few photos for the website while it's quiet," I announced.

"Great. I'll refill the toppings," Allie said.

"I'll help!" Sierra quickly offered.

A few months ago Allie might have been upset that I was taking pictures instead of helping with the toppings. But ever since her mom made me the unofficial social media director of the shop, she doesn't mind as much. I make all the updates to the Molly's Ice Cream website. I upload photos to the shop's social media accounts, and I respond to any messages or comments people post. I don't mind doing it, because Mrs. S. is so busy making the ice cream and keeping the shop running seven days a week that it would never get done. Also it's a lot of fun!

I walked up to Sophie and her mom. "Would you mind if I took a photo of your daughter with the sundae and post it on our website?" I asked. "We'll identify her by first name only."

"Of course!" the mom replied. She pulled a napkin from the dispenser. "I should clean up her face first, though."

"No, it's perfect, trust me!" I said. Sophie had ice cream all over the outside of her mouth, with flecks of coconut and sprinkles stuck to it. I pointed my phone at Sophie. "Smile and say 'ice cream'!"

"Ice cream!" Sophie cried, scrunching up her eyes. When she opened her mouth to smile, I noticed that she was missing her two front teeth. How cute was that? This was social media gold!

"Okay, now pick up the spoon and pretend you're going to put it into your mouth, but stop just before you get there," I instructed.

Sophie obeyed, and I snapped away.

"That was great! Thanks!" I said. "You can find the photos on the Molly's Ice Cream website."

Sophie's mom nodded, and then I moved to the dad and his two boys. I took a few shots of them eating their ice cream cones. And the teenage girls let me shoot them sipping their milkshakes with our new paper straws—aqua, to match the cushions on the chairs.

"Wait, let us see!" one of the girls demanded before I could walk away. I handed them my phone, and they huddled together, scrolling through the photos.

"Wow, these are all good!" the girl said. "You should be, like, a professional photographer or something."

"Thanks. It's part of my job," I replied. I *knew* I was good, but it was nice to hear it out loud.

No new customers had come in, so back behind the counter I began to upload the photos. First I posted them on the website, and then on the social media accounts, which were all linked, so I only had to do them once.

For Sophie, I wrote: Cute alert! Order a Bird's Nest Sundae and you'll be smiling too. #sundaysundae #icecream #MollysIceCream #Bayville #cute

For the dad and the boys: Open till 9 every Sunday! #icecream #sundaysundae #icecreamcone #Mollys-IceCream #Bayville

For the teenage girls: Milkshakes taste better with our new planet-friendly straws. #milkshake #savethe-planet #MollysIceCream #Bayville

I could have come up with at least ten more hashtags, but I heard Allie call out behind me.

"Incoming!"

A group of little girls in soccer jerseys came in with their coach. I slipped my phone back into my pocket.

"On it!" I said, and I turned on the charm with a big smile for the coach. "Welcome to Molly's. How can I help you today?"

The rush lasted for about an hour, but I had a chance to check the accounts before our shift ended and it was time to clean up.

"Wow!" I said. "Sophie's photo has forty-five likes online already."

"Who's Sophie?" Sierra asked.

"That little girl who ordered the Bird's Nest. With the two front teeth missing," I replied.

Sierra nodded. "She *was* cute!"

"Twenty-eight likes on the milkshakes," I reported. "Oh, and here's a comment: 'How late are you open tonight?'"

I rolled my eyes. "Duh. It says right in the caption that we're open till nine."

"Don't write that!" Allie warned.

"Of course not. I am the queen of social media. I know exactly what to say," I responded, and then I typed.

Open till 9. Hope to see you soon, and bring a friend!

Sierra grinned. "The queen of social media, huh? Was there an election?"

"Queens don't get elected. They are born," I pointed out. "And anyway, I am killing it with the website and the other accounts. Molly's has a legit social media presence now. Kai says we're on the way to becoming a recognizable brand."

Kai is my business-obsessed older brother. I get a lot of good advice from him.

I checked out the photo of the family eating ice cream cones. "Okay, now here's a sensible comment. 'How come your chocolate ice cream tastes so much better than the kind I make at home?'"

Mrs. S. walked into the room as I was saying this. "Wow, that's flattering. So what kind of thing do you say to respond to a comment like that?"

I thought for a minute. "How about this?" I said, and I read out loud as I typed. "Don't even *try* to duplicate it. Why torture yourself and waste time and money trying to make it at home? Life is short! Come to Molly's and enjoy all the best tasting chocolate ice cream you want!"

Everybody laughed.

"That is perfect," Mrs. S. said. "People tell me they love following Molly's on social media, not just to see what's new, but to see 'Molly's' funny responses. You are a star, Tamiko!"

"Actually, she's a queen. Queen of social media," Allie corrected, laughing.

"All right, I was just kidding before," I said. "I might be good at social media, but I'm not exactly a star."

"Even kids at school treat you like you're a celebrity," Sierra said.

"No, they don't," I protested.

She turned to Allie and her mom. "People stop by our table at lunch and compliment her on the website. Even *Eeee*-wan," she teased.

I rolled my eyes. Earlier in the year Ewan and I got paired up in art class, and we had to draw each other's portraits. I wasn't exactly psyched about it because he's a popular kid who hangs out with a bunch of jerks. But it turns out he's not a jerk—he's nice and a really good artist, and I ended up drawing a lot of pictures of him in different styles. So *of course* Sierra and Allie assumed that means I have a crush on him, and they've been torturing me about it forever.

It's kind of annoying. They're my friends, and I love them, but just because they're obsessing about boys all the time doesn't mean I have to. I have no interest in dating right now. And so what if sometimes my stomach does this weird flip when I pass by him in the hallway? That doesn't mean I have a crush on him, all right?

Allie walked over with one of those pointy paper cups that you put on the end of your ice cream cone to prevent drips, and placed it on top of my head, giggling.

"I crown thee Tamiko, Queen of Social Media!" she said. "What is thy command?"

"I command you to stop calling me the queen of social media," I said, taking the paper cone off my head. "I'm sorry I ever brought it up."

Allie's face got thoughtful. "You know, Tamiko, now that you have a following, you should maybe create a blog of your own. You know, do something more than just post friend stuff on SuperSnap. You could post photos of all the stuff you create."

I liked the sound of that. "I'm not sure why I never thought of that before," I admitted. "But I like it. I could post outfits I've made and get people to rate them and stuff."

"You could even do videos," Sierra suggested.

Mrs. S. nodded. "I think that's a wonderful idea," she said. "It's never too early to start thinking about your future. And a successful website would be a wonderful thing to show to prospective colleges in a few years. It will be here quicker than you expect!"

"I didn't even think of that," I said. "I love these ideas. Thanks!"

"Now, if you girls don't mind cleaning the tables, I'll get your pay for this week," Mrs. S. said, and she headed to the back room of the shop.

We cleaned up the tables and divided up the tips we'd gotten that afternoon. I heard a beep and saw Mom outside in her car.

"Need a ride, Sierra?" I asked. "You can come over for dinner if you want."

"Sounds good, but I can't," she said. "I'm going straight to band practice."

"Cool," I said. "Bye!"

After getting my pay from Mrs. S., I took off my apron and headed outside. Normally, I might be mildly annoyed that Sierra had band practice—her schedule is so crazy, and she doesn't always have time to hang out with me. But that night my mind was whirring with plans.

I couldn't wait to start my blog!

Looking for another great book?
Find it
IN THE MIDDLE.

Fun, fantastic books for kids
in the in-be**TWEEN** age.

IntheMiddleBooks.com

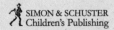

sew zoey

Zoey's clothing design blog puts her on the A-list in the fashion world . . . but when it comes to school, will she be teased, or will she be a trendsetter?